THE REVEREND AND THE PEACEMAKER

THE REVEREND AND THE PEACEMAKER

ROGER BAKER

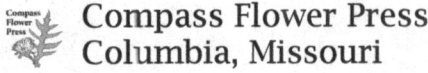

Compass Flower Press
Columbia, Missouri

Compass Flower Press
Columbia, Missouri
compassflowerpress.com

Library of Congress Control Number: 2021920989
ISBN 978-1-951960-29-2 Trade Paperback
ISBN 978-1-951960-24-7 Ebook

Chapter 1

Hunkered down in the corner of our emplacement made of wood and dirt, realizing how close death was all around us, I was thinking of home and my father. With the explosion of incoming shells and the yammer of small arms fire from almost all directions, I clutched my automatic weapon in my right hand and the old family Long Colt in my left. The old Colt wasn't as efficient as the modern rapid-fire rifle, but I felt much more safe and secure having the handgun with me.

"The name is James Riley Cole Junior. Oh, and you'd better make that Captain J. R. Cole, United States Army." During my active service I was commander of Company E, 175th Ranger group, Bien Hoa, Vietnam.

When entering the armed services I never intended to stay longer than the time required by the Selective Service Act. However, I found I enjoyed the military and did not mind or fear any of the ramifications included in active service.

After college ROTC I received my commission and rather quickly moved up the ranks. By proving I had the right stuff and with the help of the old Long Colt I achieved captaincy swiftly in my service. It being wartime also certainly helped.

Our garrison had been under attack for more than eighteen hours. It wasn't the action of a Viet Cong combat group but appeared to be a full-blown North Vietnamese offensive. Several times before, my men and I had faced

1

similar actions and most of us managed to survive. Sadly, there were always casualties. For some reason I always felt when the chips were down the old Colt appeared to even the odds.

It's strange, but the story of the old Long Colt is also a story of my family. It defended my life, my father's life, and my grandfather's life as we each served in the Army of the United States.

My grandfather carried it in the American Indian Wars of the 1870s and '80s. My father depended on it in the Great War of 1917 and '18. And it was with me from my first Vietnam combat action. It never showed a spot of wear and left in its wake some peculiar stories over the years of its combat use.

My grandfather, Samuel Doyle Cole, left his family and home in mid-Missouri in 1866 at the age of seventeen. He had been too young to enter the American Civil War, but he was not going to miss the adventure of the Indian Wars in the far west.

He enlisted in the United States Army at Jefferson Barracks in Saint Louis and was assigned to a cavalry unit that would later become part of General George Armstrong Custer's 7th Cavalry. Actually Custer was not General, but Colonel Custer. At the end of the Civil War his brevet rank of general was revoked and he returned to his actual rank of colonel. My grandfather always called him General because of his great respect for the man, and after becoming an officer myself, I felt the same way.

Over a ten-year period my grandfather would serve in the areas of Kansas and Oklahoma. He may even have seen service in Texas. By the early years of the 1870s he had become a noncom in Custer's command in Kansas. Then in 1876, it was off to Dakota Territory and the Little Bighorn. He didn't participate in the famous battle along the Little Bighorn River, having been thrown from a horse a few days prior to the massacre. He was left behind, as the 7th proceeded on its expedition toward the Bighorn Mountains and its date with destiny. An act of fate and a concussion saved his life.

However, sometime later he was on a small patrol out of Fort Abraham Lincoln in Dakota Territory when he was taken prisoner by a Lakota war party led by the young war chief, Thunder Cloud.

He never discovered why he was not immediately tortured and killed but instead was stripped of most of his uniform and boots, tied on a horse, and taken with the band. Being almost naked and barefoot, he assumed death was not too far in the future for him.

After a day or two, he and the band arrived at what appeared to be a hunting or war camp. There were areas for warrior training, care of horses, and a few permanent lodges.

For several days, while being tied to a stake in front of Thunder Cloud's lodge, he was allowed to roast in the northwestern sun by day and nearly freeze to death at night. Riding all day tied to a horse was terrible torture, but being tied to a tree or stake all night made him sometimes pray for death to end his misery.

One night as the war party was dancing and preparing for what my grandfather believed was a coming battle the next day, he discovered the bonds securing him to the stake were a little loose. Apparently the warrior assigned to tie him to the stake, being excited about the battle preparations and war dance, neglected to be sure he was securely tied. In a short time he was able to work himself free.

Chapter 2

His first impulse was to try to run, but he realized he was too weak and couldn't get far away quickly enough not to be recaptured. Also he could not run without shoes or survive without clothing. He decided to simply try to conceal himself for the night and during the coming battle attempt to slip away.

Then it struck him. Could he possibly hide in Thunder Cloud's lodge? Moving as quickly as his previously bound body would allow, he moved to the lodge opening and looked in. Though he had not seen anyone but the men in the war party, he expected to perhaps find a slave or Thunder Cloud's wife. He saw no one so he crept inside. As his eyes became accustomed to the dim firelight inside, he began to distinguish weapons of war, battle clothing, and several piles of tanned animal hides with odd pieces of white man's clothing mixed in. One pile was arranged as a sleeping pallet, which he assumed was where the chief slept.

While his eyes were becoming more accustomed to the light, his nose was picking up several different scents. The smoke from the lodge fire told him that the burning wood was mountain pine and sage. There was also the scent of cooked meat and he saw bones and remains near the fire. Then he picked up the smell of something very repugnant, the scent of old human blood, and he saw fresh scalps hanging from a war shield. In addition, there was of course the scent of animal skins. That brought his

5

attention back to the piles of cured hides around the outer wall of the lodge, and a plan came together. He could hide beneath one of the piles of skins and probably never be discovered.

As he wriggled under the animal skins he took one last glance at the war shield with the scalps, and a chill ran down his spine. One of the scalps was part black hair and part snow-white hair. The sight immediately caused him to feel sick at his stomach. The scalp was from the head of one of his old close friends, Roy Harden. In the troop he was known as Skunk, not out of disrespect but quite the opposite. Skunk was one hell of a trooper and a friend to every man. Roy encouraged the name because he had been born with part snow-white hair and part coal-black hair, and it made him unique. He invited the recognition.

Grandfather realized that Thunder Cloud was the one who harvested Roy's scalp and it turned his blood ice cold, but he knew his hair would soon join Roy's if he did not hide quickly.

As he continued to crawl under the pile of hides, he surveyed the whole lodge and decided he was following the best plan available. Near the bottom of the pile his head bumped into something cold and hard. Unable to see in the darkness under the skins he allowed his hand to do the looking. Suddenly he realized in his grasp was an army-issue long-barreled Colt revolver. His hand told him there was a gun belt and holster with a cartridge case attached, as well.

Gramps told my father he quickly stuck his head out from beneath the stack of pelts and checked the cylinder. The gun was loaded and there were extra cartridges in the case. As he ducked back under the tanned robes, Thunder Cloud entered the lodge.

Peeking out along a wrinkle in one of the hides, in the firelight he watched the young war chief prepare for sleep and the coming battle. Believing he was safely hidden, Grandfather relaxed a little, but continued to watch as Thunder Cloud lowered himself to his sleeping mat next to the fire.

Suddenly, without warning, the warrior leaped up from his sleeping spot and with a long wicked-looking blade in his hand, rushed toward Grandfather's hiding place.

Grandfather knew a blast from the big revolver would alert the entire camp and his death would be a certainty as a result, but Thunder Cloud's long blade would accomplish the same results, except he would be dead a whole lot quicker. Without more thought, Gramps raised the muzzle of the big pistol's barrel beneath the pile of skins, pointed it in the direction of Thunder Cloud's advance, thumbed back the hammer, and pulled the trigger.

Chapter 3

Grandfather immediately felt the violent recoil of the big Colt but heard no loud report. With great fear in his being, he silently questioned, *did the weapon fire?* Then he saw Thunder Cloud's head snap backward as his body crumpled to the lodge floor in death.

For a short while, Gramps lay where he was in maddening fear and listened for the camp to come awake and rush for Thunder Cloud's lodge, but he heard no sound except his own fearful breathing. As Grandfather slowly crept on hands and knees from beneath the heap of skins, he again puzzled, *did the Colt not make a sound when it fired?* He could not supply a reasonable answer, but he knew he had to run before the camp discovered the young war chief was dead.

He carefully and silently rose from his hiding place and rapidly surveyed the entire interior of the lodge. Surprisingly he found his own uniform trousers in a pile of white man's apparel apparently taken from the dead or stolen in some raid. Grandfather quickly dressed in his trousers and a checkered flannel shirt from the pile. He fastened the gun belt around his waist and slipped the Colt into the holster. Then he remembered to replace the spent cartridge that had killed Thunder Cloud.

He was still barefoot, so he gave the surroundings another look in hopes of finding a pair of moccasins big enough to fit. He knew he could not travel far without something to protect his feet from the sharp rocks and thorns. Then he saw the toe of an army boot sticking out from beneath another pile of hides. He prayed that there were two and that they would fit. Hurriedly kicking the pile of hides aside he discovered that luck was with him once more. There were two and they were his own boots. Not taking time to look for socks, he put the boots on and prepared to leave.

Suddenly a new thought struck his mind. Realizing he was facing the cold of the night, he picked up a blanket from the piles of hides and clothing. Carefully folding it as small as possible and tying it with a strip of leather, he slung it over his shoulder.

Without further consideration he peeked out the lodge opening. Seeing no one, he crept noiselessly into the totally wild blackness of the surrounding high plains.

Not knowing which direction was the best way to safety, he decided anywhere else was probably better than being close to the war party's camp, so he started walking rapidly, and running a little in the direction he was facing. He saw the North Star almost directly to his left, so he believed he was probably headed east—toward civilization and safety. If he was not headed east he would know for sure in a few hours when the sun rose.

After what seemed like a thousand hours, the light of dawn shone on the horizon directly in front of him. He realized he had made the right decision earlier, so he just continued his walk in the direction of friendly faces. When full daylight began showing brightly, he began to look for a place to hide. He would stay quiet until after sundown. Then he could continue his hike to freedom. He was feeling the need for food and more importantly water, but he would just have to do without until darkness.

He settled down near the top of a rocky outcropping to hide until nightfall when he could continue onward to safety. Untying the sand-colored blanket, he lay back, covered himself, and prepared for as long a nap as he would be allowed.

Then he heard the sound of gunfire from a short distance away. Carefully rising up and looking over the rocks in front of him, he saw dust and movement about a hundred and fifty yards to his front in another rocky area. Changing his position a little, he observed a small group of cavalrymen below him, penned down by a larger band of Lakota warriors between himself and the troopers.

He contemplated remaining hidden until the fight was over but could not bear to see his fellow troopers being wiped out to save his own life. He quickly considered his best course of action and how he could be of assistance in the fight. Then he remembered one of General Custer's axioms, "Success favors the bold." With that thought in mind he slowly and quietly inched forward and down from his hiding place and into a position directly in the rear of the attacking braves.

When he knew he had arrived in range of the big Colt's power, he settled once more into a defendable hiding place where he could see most of the warriors clearly. He said he was a little surprised that the warriors were not attacking on horseback, but after a little more consideration he realized the landscape did not lend itself to a mounted attack.

Allowing the big revolver to have its own way, he commenced a deliberate and deadly rate of fire. After six shots and six fewer aggressors he was forced to pause to reload. As he was refueling the pistol, some of the warriors stood up to try to pinpoint his position and were immediately dispatched by the Trapdoor Springfield carbines being fired by the entrapped cavalrymen. After a couple more cylinders of fire from the big Colt, the war party became completely disorganized. Within a few minutes, the warriors still able made a mad run to the place where their horses were hobbled and rapidly rode away, but there were far fewer leaving than had started the battle.

The cavalry troopers, after a short pause, spread out over the area, checking their own dead and wounded and assuring that the Indian bodies on the ground were dead or incapacitated.

Grandfather cautiously made his way down out of the rocks and approached the troop as the men were once more forming into a military unit. There he discovered the troop was commanded by a Lieutenant Fuller, a new replacement in the 7th Cavalry.

After telling his story he was given some trail rations and cool water, and assigned a horse that had belonged to one of the men killed in the scrimmage. They decided two bodies could be tied over the saddle of one horse, allowing my grandfather a mount of his own.

As he rode back to the post with the troop, he felt badly about the loss of two more of his fellow cavalrymen, but at the same time he was thankful he had survived. The ride also gave him time to contemplate the mystery of the service Colt.

Chapter 4

The past came alive with a form of wonder as word passed of the Lakota ambush and the one-man relief party. The small troop of survivors could not believe one man, with one hand weapon, could wreak so much havoc on a seasoned Indian war party. Grandfather was also filled with wonder at the ease of handling and the degree of accuracy of the mysterious firearm. At the same time he was very thankful that it was in his possession.

The quartermaster checked the gun's serial number against the pistols listed in his record books to determine if it had belonged to a trooper who had been killed or captured by the Indians, but no number match could be found. There were numbers close to the old gun's, but no match. Because it was not found to be the property of the US government, my grandfather was allowed to retain possession.

Gramps was embarrassed when the colonel praised him in front of the entire post command for his bravery in action. Everyone congratulated him but no one believed he had killed Thunder Cloud to make his escape. They believed Thunder Cloud was just too great a warrior for one trooper to be able to kill him in a face-to-face contest. The disbelief did not bother grandfather. He was only glad that he was still standing and Thunder Cloud was not. He also reported that Skunk was confirmed dead. The entire troop received that news in a very somber manner.

13

Grandfather stayed in the cavalry for several more years until another horse accident brought an end to his military career. That time a horse was shot from under him in a running battle. The dying horse fell on his right leg, breaking it in three places. Gramps healed after a time, but with a stiff leg he could no longer mount a horse quickly, so he was forced to retire from the cavalry and the frontier.

In a short time he returned to the region of his birth and worked with horses and tack for many more years.

In 1898, at the age of forty-nine, he married a young widow, Maggie Jane Riley Day, a few years his junior, and in 1900, my father was born.

Grandfather lived until 1923 and died at the age of seventy-four. My father was twenty-three and had fought in France in 1918 before he lost his father.

14

Chapter 5

My father was raised in the same little Missouri town, Boonville, where my grandfather met and married my grandmother. He worked on the river, in some small factories in town, and on farms in the surrounding areas.

My father, James Riley Cole Senior, like my grandfather, joined the army when the nation called for its young men to become soldiers to fight another war. And again, like his father before him, he found a fondness for the military. He entered the service with the plan to remain a fighting man for the rest of his life. However, the United States was only in the war-fighting business from late 1917 until November 1918, when the war ended. Armistice Day was celebrated November 11, 1918.

Because of the mystery of the old Colt, and because my grandfather believed it was blessed with the power to protect and assist its owner, he gave it to my father and insisted he carry it as a sidearm if he went into combat.

My father left the old belt, holster, and cartridge case behind. He had a new belt and holster made for the old weapon.

Early in 1918 he arrived in France and was reassigned to the 35th Division, and in August he found himself on the Eastern Front. Most of his time was spent in the trenches, with almost daily advances over the top into no-man's-land. He found the big side weapon a mind-soothing companion as he faced the constant threat of death from German machine guns and artillery.

15

More than once the old long-barreled .45 seemed to sense hidden danger before it came into view. My father told me many tales of drawing the big pistol from its holster for no apparent reason, then almost immediately needing it for defense against some enemy incursion.

The first time it happened he was returning, via the trenches, from a period on guard post to his sleeping accommodations in a log- and earth-covered bunker. It was late at night, and he was almost walking in his sleep as he trudged past the mouth of a cross trench and stumbled on toward his bunk. Suddenly the old Colt fairly leaped into his hand as he turned and looked back into the shadowed mouth of the cross trench. A large man in a long gray coat raised a trench knife above his head in a downward stabbing pose. My father said he felt the recoil of the big weapon but never heard a barking report. The big man's head jerked, and he toppled back into the mouth of the cross trench. My father silently questioned why he did not hear a sound and also how he saw the man in almost total darkness. But he could smell the burnt powder as the smoke escaped from the muzzle of the long barrel. Father said he then waited, watched, and listened for a minute or two to be sure the man had been alone. Then he proceeded on his way.

Continuing on down the trench, my father did not go into his bunker but went on to the command bunker to report the incident to the officer on duty.

Grabbing a lantern, the officer and another guard accompanied my father back to the cross trench where they found a dead German with a killing wound to the left side of his head. The trench knife was found under his body.

A dead German was not a big deal in the trenches, but when it was evident that he had died from a gunshot wound, everyone close by wondered why they had not heard the sound of the shot. My father could not clarify the reason either. The magnificent old pistol once more presented its mysterious actions. That time it was my father who was thankful for its presence, even if he could not explain all that had happened.

16

Chapter 6

During the following weeks before the armistice, more unexplainable events took place, and the old Colt was always front and center in the action.

One of the incidents was perhaps not that unusual, but it was still pretty much unbelievable to anyone familiar with military weapons. The Springfield Model 1903 was the accepted US Army weapon of the day in 1918, and it would prove to be an extremely accurate combat rifle for many years that followed. But one of the strange events that took place was the killing of a German sniper.

One morning my father and one of his buddies were moving along a trench from one observation point to another. For just a moment the other man raised his head a little above the top of the trench timbers, probably to take a quick look toward the German lines. The buddy slumped and tumbled into the bottom of the trench. Then my father heard the crack of a rifle shot. His buddy had a bullet wound in the forehead. An observer with a periscope said he saw the smoke from the rifle but could not see the sniper. Several soldiers with their 1903 Springfield rifles fired a volley into the area of the muzzle smoke, but it appeared to have no effect.

Once more the old handgun seemed to appear in my father's hand. Climbing over the logs out of the trench with tears in his eyes and curse words flowing from his mouth, he stood up in clear sight of the sniper. As a shot rang out from the sniper's rifle, my father flinched a little,

17

and then the old pistol belched two tongues of flame from its muzzle. At a distance that was almost the limit for a rifle, the sniper stood straight up and then fell sideways over a pile of destroyed timber from a previous artillery strike and moved no more. It was later discovered that my father had a small burn blister on the upper edge of his left ear. The sniper's bullet had been that close to scoring a double killing that morning. The Colt had done its job once again. It was as if the big handgun had a mind of its own. It was later determined that the two rounds fired had traveled at least one hundred and seventy-five yards.

Sometime later, while on a patrol, my father was credited with taking down five German soldiers who were hiding in ambush in a destroyed building along a secluded roadway. Because of a foot blister, my father had fallen behind the other men as they moved cautiously along the shadowed trail. After the men had passed the ruins of the old house, five German soldiers crept out of the debris and fell in a short distance behind the patrol. My father, gripping the big Colt and seeing what was about to happen, stayed out of sight in the shadows. When the Germans stopped and took aim at the backs of the American troops, the mysterious old gun moved into action. My father took slow and deliberate aim, and he commenced to fire five quick shots, leaving five German bodies in the roadway.

Father's rifle was still slung over his left shoulder.

Still later in the war as the fighting settled into almost total trench warfare, it was unusual to see any buildings left standing in no-man's-land, but one afternoon, father and seven or eight other soldiers were sent over the top to attempt to visually locate a machine-gun emplacement that was doing great damage in their sector.

As they crept and crawled over the seeming moonscape they came upon the ruins of what had once been a two-story stone structure. Though the windows were gone, through the window holes partial walls could still be seen standing inside.

As the small group moved forward toward the structure, they came under heavy machine-gun fire. Two or three of the men went down immediately, while others found cover a little distance short of the ruins. Father was closer to the old house and was able to make his way inside. Finding a secure corner in the stone walls with debris piled in front, he slid into a small space that appeared to be defensible. He could see a hundred and eighty degrees to the front and up a partially destroyed staircase to what little remained of the second floor. He could hear the men outside defending themselves from their various places of concealment, but he had no way of knowing how many were still in the fight.

As Father waited for the battle to come to him, he continuously surveyed the terrain in all directions, even over his shoulder and out the rear of the destroyed structure.

Then, through a smaller hole in the wall behind him, he saw five or six German soldiers advancing toward the rear of the house. Realizing that he could not move his rifle freely in the tight space where he was hidden, he chose the old reliable Colt to defend himself. Having confidence in the hand weapon and his ability to use it, he waited for the adversaries to come into his line of fire.

Shortly, a German soldier stepped through a hole in what had once been a solid rear wall, apparently concentrating on the fight outside the front of the building. When he reached a window hole and peered out, Father allowed the big revolver to have its way. The enemy soldier was driven forward through the opening, half-in and half-out of the window hole.

As Father was involved with the first German, another entered through the same opening and evidently seeing the muzzle smoke from the old gun, snapped a quick shot at the pile of rubble. Father fired back and another enemy soldier went down.

Suddenly there was firing from all directions, even from the partial floor above. Father decided the men above him were the greater threat, so he concentrated on the area over his head. As he once more waited for another target, he reloaded the big Colt. He then saw the toe of a boot sticking out from behind a small section of plastered wall above. This time, taking careful aim, he fired through the chalky wall about five feet above the boot toe. He heard a solid thud and saw the sole of a boot where the toe had been. Father immediately returned his attention back to the dangers in front and toward both sides and continued to keep up a steady flow of .45 caliber rounds, pausing only to refuel the old revolver.

Abruptly the surroundings became silent. Father remained hidden and quiet until he heard English being spoken and finally understood that someone was calling his rank and name. Calling back, he realized the little battle was over.

Two of his fellow soldiers had been killed, one wounded, and the rest were safe and well. In front of his hiding place eleven enemy soldiers were counted, ten dead and one severely wounded.

When the group finally returned to their trenches, the wounded American soldier, Private Wayne R. Berry, divulged he had observed the locations of a number of enemy machine-gun emplacements. Using Berry's intelligence, artillery was able to neutralize the enemy machine-gun nests. For his actions Private Berry was awarded the Distinguished Service Cross. Later Father discovered that trooper Berry was from a small town just a few miles from his own hometown of Boonville, Missouri.

Father continued to participate in battle until he and his fellow soldiers were no longer needed to defend freedom and our nation.

Father survived the conflict and returned home to the same house and farm his father had returned to in 1895 from the Indian Wars.

After returning from France in 1918, Father became somewhat lost in a life full of peace. He may have, as was later learned in the medical field, suffered from a stress syndrome brought on by his time in combat. Whatever the reason, for a number of years he could not settle down in one location practicing one vocation. He followed many different trails until 1945, when the Second World

War came to an end. First he became involved in the soldier's march on Washington to attempt to secure their promised bonuses for their wartime service. Next, it was an extended tour of the Dakota territory, searching for his father's military life and time of service with General Custer. Then he lived the life of a hobo, riding the rails from one great ocean to the other. Finally, he found a job in an ammunition factory in western Missouri during the years of World War II. There he met my mother, Wendy Wiley Wells, the flaming-haired beauty who stole his heart. They were wed in late 1946, then returned to the place of his birth and lived in the same house where he was born. It was the same house where I would arrive in 1947, when he was forty-seven years old and Mother was thirty-two.

Chapter 7

As my thoughts moved in and out of home and history, I remained aware of the action around me. Then over the noise of battle I heard the sound of aircraft overhead.

Ten Huey helicopter gunships appeared and their firepower broke up the attack. My grandfather's army Colt and seeming mystic powers were spared duty, but even so, three of my men were killed, two wounded, and the whole crew of one of the ten Hueys was lost when it was shot down. In country every win at the end of an action was a good win, but at the same time there were a hell of a lot of tears attached.

I carried the old sidearm religiously and it proved to be the difference in many firefights. However, a day came when I was ordered to take a fast-moving patrol into a lowland jungle to intercept and destroy a Viet Cong unit before it could link up with a regular North Vietnamese battle group attempting to move into our sector. Since we would be moving fast, I would need to travel as lightly equipped as possible. I decided to leave the old Colt's holster, belt, and cartridge case behind in the care of the quartermaster. I simply slipped the revolver and a few extra rounds into the bottom of my backpack.

Fifteen handpicked men from my company and I geared up and left on the mission. We were several miles into the jungle and close to the border of our sector when we realized we were too late to prevent the linkup of the two enemy groups. We had just cut the trail of the

23

combined force when all hell broke loose. We were almost immediately hit by the entire combined force.

Being pinned down we could neither advance nor withdraw. We called for air support and were told it would be ten to fifteen minutes before the arrival of any relief. Then we realized we were in heavy jungle surroundings and the overhead canopy would block us from aerial view. We told Command that when the aircrafts were over us, we would fire a rocket flare straight up to show our location. Standard operating procedure was for the aircraft to then drop ordnance fifty to one hundred yards out from the flare in a complete circle. Being hit by that friendly fire was definitely a possible consequence, but the situation we were in did not leave many other alternatives. By the time the relief aircrafts arrived overhead the majority of my fifteen men were down, but I did not know their conditions. The flare was fired and the explosive ordnance began to burst all around us. Suddenly I felt a hot burning sensation around my head and then—nothing.

Chapter 8

After a few moments I opened my eyes and did not understand what I was looking at. The jungle canopy was gone and the sunlight was so bright it blinded me. I tried to raise my hand to my face to shield my eyes from the sunlight, but I could not move my arm. Then I realized I was lying on a soft surface. The sunlight suddenly dimmed and I saw a face looking down into mine.

"Captain Cole. Can you hear me?"

I heard my voice reply, "Yes Sir." Before the face could say more, I asked, "Where am I?"

"You're in the 45th surgical field hospital. You have a head wound. But now that you are awake, we should be able to transfer you to a hospital in Saigon."

"How long have I been here?"

"Almost a week, but we were afraid to move you while you were still unconscious."

"I can't move my arms. Am I paralyzed?"

"No, we have you restrained so you would not hurt yourself while you were unconscious."

"How are my men?"

"I'm sorry, you will have to ask someone from Command when you are well enough to make your official report."

Then once more there was nothing as I slipped back into unconsciousness.

But again, I opened my eyes and I could see I was all alone in a room with the sound of various machines running above my head. I could move my arms and legs, but my head felt like it weighed a ton, and I realized my head was wrapped and taped heavily from my eyes up.

Then someone entered the room. I couldn't move my head, so I waited until they looked down into my face. Then I asked, "How am I?"

The face above me said, "I'm Doctor Blade, and you are recovering, we think. But you need to be examined by a neurologist before we will know how badly you have been injured."

"How are my men?"

"I'm sorry. You will have to be debriefed by Command and they will answer your questions pertaining to your last firefight.

The doctor excused himself and I was left to my own distractions.

In a few more days, a man in uniform with the rank of colonel came to my room. He said, "I'm Doctor Tobius, and I'm a neurologist. I'll be testing you for the possible loss of mental acuity."

First, he asked questions pertaining to my life prior to military service, such as my full name, my birth date, and the same for my parents. I had no trouble with that. Next, he talked about our nation and its political structure. Again, no problem. Then it was a review of my military career. Once again, no problem. Last he had me do some simple physical activities, such as finger touching, eye and facial movements, and then he had me do some physical and verbal activities in reverse.

Then as he stood up to leave, he asked, "Now is there anything you would like to ask me?"

Almost in a state of total frustration I once more asked, "How are my men?"

Now it was his turn to appear either frustrated or hurt, as he dropped his eyes. "You are the only survivor of your last mission."

Hot tears welled up in my eyes and I gagged as my stomach convulsed violently. "No, No, No!" I screamed as nurses rushed into the room. Then a long mournful final

"No" escaped my lips, and I cried as though I would never be able to stop.

The doctor excused himself, but as he left the room, he turned and said, "I'll make arrangements for you to talk to another officer and he will conduct your debriefing."

For several days I did not eat, and I slept very little.

One doctor asked me if I wanted to talk to a counselor.

I told him, "Not until some son of a bitch comes and debriefs me!"

The next morning a brigadier general appeared in my room with a noncom carrying a recording machine. I did not salute and he immediately started the debriefing.

"Captain Cole. Tell me everything you remember about the last firefight you were involved in."

I told him I was ordered to choose fifteen of the best men in my company to conduct an intercept and destroy mission against a Viet Cong unit before it could link up with a larger North Vietnamese battle group, that Command indicated they believed the group, if combined, would attack our entire sector. For whatever reason, we were too late to prevent the linkup, and before we even had time to radio back that information, we came under a heavy attack by the combined force. I explained that we did then radio and requested air support. We were told it would be ten to fifteen minutes before support arrival. I told Command we would fire a flare out of the jungle canopy directly above our location so ordnance could be dropped around us for protection until it either broke the attack or we could sustain a counterattack. After we heard and saw the relief aircrafts, we fired the flare. I ordered my radio operator to hunker down in place as I moved out a little to check on my troops. Then I was hit and remembered nothing more.

After the general thought a moment he said, "Captain. What I'm about to tell you is not necessarily what happened after you were wounded, but it is what Command believes happened. Your story is very close to the same thing the air support commander said in his debriefing, and since you were unconscious, you cannot confirm or dispute Command's beliefs. All indications are that when the ordnance began to fall around your group, you were hit by a stray piece of shrapnel, or an enemy bullet grazed your head. At the same time, your men were collecting in the center of the ordnance drop preparing for the counterattack or evacuation. One of the enemy soldiers got close enough to throw a satchel charge into the group and all were killed. Then the entire enemy group, less their dead, simply melted away into the jungle. When the relief group landed close by and troops worked their way to your unit's location, all they found were enemy bodies, the bodies of your men, and you, a little distance away and unconscious."

Once more grief overcame me and I began to cry.

As the general finished collecting his papers and the noncom completed his work on the recorder, the general said, "I know it is of little value to you as you try to come to some semblance of acceptance of all that has happened, but I want you to know that you and your men's mission was an extreme success. After the ordnance drop, both the Viet Cong and North Vietnamese battle-groups scattered like scared animals and have not been located since. Command has not been able to determine a reason why an enemy group of that size became so scared they totally fell apart on the battlefield."

For several more days I took very little food and could not stop crying.

A counselor came to my room one afternoon and talked with me for three or four hours. He said I was suffering from depression and I needed some antidepressant medication to regain my mental control. They did very little good for my condition.

Sometime later a Catholic priest came into my room to talk. I explained that I was Protestant, not Catholic. But he said, "We are all children of the same God and I will talk to you about God, without adding any church doctrine.

I listened and he talked of war and how both good men and bad men die in a pitch battle. He continued, "And we have to be able to let them go when it happens, the good to God and the bad to Satan. If there was not bad in the world we would not need God. And we both know we must have God in our hearts or we will not survive. I'm not talking about life, but about eternity. And you do understand God wants to be a part of every activity we are involved in, from brushing our teeth to tying our shoes." Then the look on his face changed a little. "You do realize that sometimes bad men become better or good men in the heat of battle, and God protects their souls also."

Then a thought entered my mind. I wondered if God had protected me in all of my previous combat or was it the old Colt?

I asked the priest, "Can a man be watched over and protected by an earthly item?"

He answered, "Only if God commanded it to be."

Suddenly, I felt a new feeling go through my body. I realized I had to have more answers than the priest had time or perhaps knowledge to provide.

Chapter 9

Almost overnight I began to gain on my depression, because my mind had to know the whole story of the old Colt. Was it possessed of God or had my grandfather, my father, and then I, been only lucky in combat? To answer my questions I would need to do a lot of research, but I also remembered I had the sidearm with me in the last firefight and it had still been a disaster.

At the same time, I decided to research my religion. I wanted to find God, know Him, study His teachings, and attempt to understand how the massacre of my command fit into His plan for them and me.

As I steadily regained my physical and mental acuities I began to form a plan for the future, and Captain Cole was not a part of that plan. I decided to resign my commission and concentrate on what the will of God was for me. The rest of my command did not understand how a dedicated army officer could give up his career over a simple discussion about God, but I knew my needs were much deeper than a simple military career.

Before my resignation became official, perhaps as a way of belittling my decision, a few of my fellow officers and some of my friends began to address me as Reverend Cole. As an officer I could have called them up on charges for such a breach of military courtesy, but instead I hoped they recognized a change in my personality. And if they did, it pleased me.

31

When my request to resign was approved, I noticed on the approval letter a small statement saying my resignation was approved because of possible mental deficiencies brought on by a serious head injury sustained during a combat mission.

Before I left, the old Catholic priest came to visit me one last time. He wished me luck in my search for God and gave me a small but great gift. He presented me with an old King James Version of the Bible and said, "Captain Cole, this Bible was carried by one of my fellow chaplains. He was a Protestant and a great man. He was killed in combat in Korea as he was doing God's will. As you read through the book, you may find drops of his blood, because he was reading to a wounded soldier when he was shot and killed. It was given to me by his company commander as a way to remember that God's work is more important to some men than life itself. Carry it and remember God is always with you, even into eternity."

I thanked him as he turned and walked away.

I returned home to Missouri without a steady income and with only plans for some simple ministry to God. I was welcomed home by my father and a few friends, but the majority of the home folk had come to believe that the war in Vietnam was the doings of the soldiers themselves, that we wanted to be there to kill and destroy. The politicians played it shrewdly as they received little or no blame for the war.

I quietly located a small shed behind the home of a trusted friend and moved in. It wasn't much, really, but about all I could afford and I believed God would provide.

A little later I learned I was entitled to a military pension from the government because of that little statement about a mental deficiency caused by a head injury in combat, but it didn't change my approach to my new life as I remained housed in the little building. I really knew God had great plans for me.

Chapter 10

Then the thought returned to me. First, I had to know all about my grandfather's old Colt pistol. In reality it did not look like an old gun. It did not have a wear mark on it and it functioned as if had been manufactured just a short time before. As I counted back the years, I suddenly realized it was about one hundred years old.

After talking to some local gun collectors, I learned I could contact Colt Patent Firearms Company and they could probably, for a price, check their historical records and perhaps shed some light on the old gun's nativity. And maybe, if I was really lucky, they would have the name and address of the original owner and when the pistol was purchased. I quickly wrote a letter to the Colt Company with the serial number and the year my grandfather became the owner.

As I began my search for God in the Bible and in other religious books and by attending services at various churches in the area, I waited for Colt's reply.

In a month or two I received a reply telling me their fee for the information they had on the old relic. I rushed to the bank and purchased a money order for the amount and quickly sent it in return mail.

As I returned to my godly research, which also included studying various commentaries on religious beliefs and doctrines, I patiently waited for the information from Colt. After another couple of weeks, I found in my mailbox an impressive eight-and-one-half by eleven-inch envelope with Colt's address and logo on the front. Inside were two typed pages of history pertaining to the old Peacemaker. I had learned from one of the gun collectors that on the American frontier, or in the old west, the long Colt had acquired that title.

The pages of information began with a paragraph thanking me for my interest in a vintage Colt product. Then the bomb shell exploded! The letter continued, "Dear Colt customer, your request for information concerning a vintage .45-caliber Colt army revolver, serial number 130175, is an unusual request, as that weapon does not exist."

I shook my head as I reviewed the serial number, heavily stamped into the frame of the weapon, 130175. I had not made a mistake. It was the same serial number I had quoted in my request.

The commentary from Colt continued, "The firearm you are referring to was removed from a shipment to be delivered to the US Army cavalry on the American western frontier in late 1875. The army Colt with that serial number was removed from an order of one hundred fifty contracted to the army. Because of several flaws in its craftsmanship and function, that serial number was never refilled and never left Colt's manufacturing plant. In our records it is listed as being destroyed. There is always the possibility that some of the parts could have been salvaged and used in other weapons. However, our records do not list a frame with that serial number as being shipped anywhere from our manufacturing plant."

Chapter 11

With no absolute satisfaction from the research on the old Colt, I returned to my studies of God and religion. Believing I did not need the mysterious hand weapon at that time, I rented a safety deposit box in one of the local banks and deposited the Colt, its vintage belt, holster, and cartridge case in it.

Slowly my understanding of God's teaching from the Bible and other religious writings increased my belief in God, and I felt a need for some definite church doctrine.

As I studied, I also began to develop a different outlook about my grandfather's old Peacemaker—that it was not the answer to all of my social problems, nor could it solve the problems that society was facing at the time. I began to think of my grandfather's old sidearm as simply a family heirloom, not the answer to settling disputes concerning differences of opinions. I felt I would never need its services for personal protection or to settle any grievances ever again. And with that outlook on life I started out to find a place to practice God's work.

However, finding a place to practice my new faith was not as easy as I had envisioned. I felt I was supposed to preach, but my past kept boiling up in front of my face every time I found a church that needed extra help.

Everything would go well for a while and then someone would ask why I left a rewarding military career Then someone else would make the accusation that I was a coward and could not face combat any longer and ran away

35

from my duty. Or it would come to light that my records said I was nothing but a mental case and the congregation did not want "a crazy" teaching them or their children. I even began to receive threats to my life and well-being. Having served in combat, I was not fearful, but the threats and innuendos hurt. Then one evening someone threw a rock with a note around it through my window. The note said, "Next time I will be a burning torch." After that, in all reality I was scared to be seen or heard around people. Though I did not want to believe it, I decided I once more needed the old Colt just to defend myself. As I retrieved the old weapon from the safety deposit box, I was so ashamed. I couldn't understand what God wanted of me.

Chapter 12

Though I felt very bad about it, the old Colt once more became a solace in my life. I could not believe that people would treat a man trying to do God's work the way I was being treated. Then the old priest's words filtered back, "There is both good and bad, not necessarily evil, all around us in the world, and we must believe that God will lead and protect."

I began looking for a place to move. Not a new house, but a new location, far enough away from where I was that I would not be readily known. However, for a time I just settled in and played the hermit and continued to study God's word.

One night, as I studied extremely late, I saw a blood spot as I thumbed through the old Bible I was given. As I looked closer, it caused me to become dizzy and very weary. I closed my eyes for a second to try to stop the dizzy feeling. When I opened my eyes, I found I had laid my head down on my arm on the table and fallen sound asleep.

Something was under my arm and when I raised it from the table, to my surprise the old Colt was on the table lying across the pages of the Bible. As my eyes came into focus, I saw the old gun rested on the first page of the first chapter of the Book of Jeremiah in the Old Testament. As I reached out to remove the old pistol from across the pages of the Bible, I felt extreme heat in the metal. It was not cool to the touch as I expected. I was fascinated and

37

frightened at the same time. Was the old relic trying to tell me something? Then I felt compelled to read the words the old gun directed me to.

In the chapter, Jeremiah, a prophet of God, was being directed by God to warn all of Ju'dah that they had forsaken Him and that all the houses of Is'ra-el would be destroyed for their iniquities. Jeremiah was so afraid! But God said for Jeremiah to go and tell the people, the pastors, and the false prophets of their wickedness and God would protect him as he spoke the words.

As I read, a feeling of wonder came over me. Was God directing me to become a prophet of some sort? Was I to lead some type of movement in God's name? I, like Jeremiah, was scared and did not know what to do. But unlike with Jeremiah, God was not speaking directly to me in my ears or putting words into my mouth. I decided to be patient and wait for God to direct me as to what He wanted me to do. I was sure He would make His wishes clear to me when and if the time and place was right for me to act. But I still felt I needed to leave where I was and go to some other place to try to preach.

A little while later I packed up my meager belongings and put them into the old Chevy station wagon I had purchased when I got my first pension check.

I made sure the old Colt was safely stowed away so if I was stopped by some law enforcement officer I would not be arrested.

I didn't know where I was headed, but I felt God would lead me where He wanted me to go to do His work. My father thought I was making a mistake by leaving, but my friends said it was the right thing to do. I felt they were relieved that I was going.

As I turned onto the highway out of town, I felt a weight rise from my shoulders, and I knew God was in the seat next to me.

After a couple of days on the road I felt I was far enough away from mid-Missouri that I could once more attempt to do God's work without people knowing my background.

Being in the southeastern part of the United States, I believed I was in the part of the nation known as the Bible Belt. I thought I might be able to work as a servant of God and not be ridiculed. But even being in that area, I decided to keep the faithful old pistol loaded and ready.

After several days of driving through the south I finally found a Protestant church in the small town of Rumble Creek, Alabama, that had a small congregation but no pastor. I questioned a few people and found a man who seemed to have some connection to the church's lay leadership that could talk to me about becoming the little church's lay minister.

I was invited to meet with the recognized elders of the church for an interview about the chances of being their minister. When we were all gathered in one of the small classrooms in the back of the church, we exchanged names and made the necessary introductions. I decided to state my name as J. R. Cole in hopes that my life's history would not catch up with me until I had the chance to present my abilities as a minister and pastor. The head of the lay group was Morgan Sedwick, the owner and operator of the corner pharmacy. John Bates owned the hardware store and Raymond Hope the general store. There were others but I could not remember their names. I felt I would get to know them as we worked together in church. After the introductions, it was on to more important pieces of business.

Of course their first inquiry was what I would expect for a salary. My reply was that I was a disabled army veteran and my pension would pay my salary. All I needed was a small place to live that I could afford to rent. They said there was a small house that went with the church as a parsonage and I could live there rent free if I would pay the utilities. The committee and I decided the arrangement was satisfactory to both parties.

Then I asked what special doctrine they expected to be followed in their services. The only doctrine they demanded was honesty, morality, and the word of God. I agreed I could preach to those requirements.

As I conversed with the members that were on the committee, I immediately felt a strong relation to one of the ladies. No, she was not a young lady that would have attracted my male interest. She was a much older lady who would pass for everyone's grandmother. She was small, appeared to be quite spry, and a total delight to visit and talk with. I knew I would grow to love her as if she were my own grandmother. Her name was Effie Stokes, and I knew I would have no trouble remembering her name. She was the one who asked me if I would like to tour the entire church. When I said yes, she took me through the old meeting house.

Much later I would learn her full name was Effinetta Ann Broyles Stokes. Her family and her husband's family were some of the early settlers in the Rumble River Valley, and both families were very successful in business.

The old building was exactly what one would expect a one-hundred-year-old church in the south to look like. It was a rectangular pine shiplap-covered building under a single roof with a bell tower reaching for Heaven. The shiplap had turned a rustic brown color with age that added a historic appearance to the old worship center. A small office was situated behind the front wall of the sanctuary with a hallway along one side, a ladder to the tower, and a door to the outside. There was a wide hall to the outside leading directly out of the center of the rear of the sanctuary, with a classroom on each side of the hall. I knew I could grow to love the old church.

I had been asked if I could stay in a motel for a couple of days while some of the women of the church gave the little parsonage a good cleaning and airing out, as it had not been lived in for an extended length of time. I mentioned seeing several motels back down the road by the river and said I could check there. But one of the church members in the group said motels in Rumble River were more expensive than the little one in Rumble Creek. After seeing my old car and how I was dressed, I supposed they thought cheaper was better for me, so I moved into the only small motel in town for a few days and the women went to work.

I was surprised they did not ask me to deliver a sermon for the church body to hear before I was hired. But if they did not like what they later heard, all it would cost them was a cleaning of the parsonage, which it must have needed even if I had not been hired.

When the day was announced for me to move into the little house, all of the members came to say hello, and they all brought food, toiletries, or linens as gifts. I asked God to help me give the best sermons that could be given and allow me to be the best pastor they ever had, because I believed this was going to be my church and my home.

Chapter 13

After living in Rumble Creek for a little while I began to wonder why there were two distinct names for an area that should probably only support one title. Why was there a town of Rumble Creek so close to a town named Rumble River?

One day Effie invited me to her house for lunch to discuss some church business. After lunch and during our discussion I mentioned the name question to her. With a small giggle she began to tell me a story. "Brother J. R., the story of the two names should be very simple, but in reality it is somewhat complex. First, I assume you understand the topography of the two Rumbles. Rumble River was the name of the small town that sprang up beside the river of the same name early in the formative years of our nation. As the area became inhabited, less and less open land was available for building sites, so the little town began to sprawl along and away from Rumble River. As the sprawl continued, suddenly a city emerged. Eventually it touched a small water source that emptied into Rumble River. Of course that creek was called Rumble Creek. I'm sure when you first came here you noticed you came in on Rumble Creek Boulevard. Many, many years ago it was simply Rumble Creek Road. After the Civil War, as times became better money-wise, the more affluent families left Rumble River and came out along the small stream to build their nicer homes. I'm also sure you have noticed more beauty

43

exists here than closer to the river. My grandfather, when he returned from the war in 1865, purchased land here, and when he became wealthy enough, he built the house you are visiting in right now. It's called a mansion because it is big and spacious. He wanted a home like this to house his family and to impress his associates. Until the end of World War II, Rumble Creek was known as the Village. But after the war the postal service told the village fathers that a more precise name was needed. Because the village was along Rumble Creek, that was the name chosen by the town elders. So that is why we are Rumble Creek next to Rumble River, and now it all appears to be one larger town."

I thanked Effie for the story and then I was better able to understand why some of the town's citizens said they lived in Rumble River and some said Rumble Creek.

Though it was much longer, it seemed I had only lived in Rumble Creek for a few days when I received word from Missouri that my father had been called home. One of my closer friends with whom I had kept in contact called to tell me my father had passed away. Before I made an announcement to the church body, I spent the greater part of one day in the church praying for my father's soul and for my own strength and understanding. After meeting with the church elders and receiving their permission to be away from the church for a few days, I made arrangements to fly back to Boonville, Missouri to bury my father. He was the last of my immediate family, as my mother went to be with God right after I entered military service. My father's death, I felt, was the final chapter in my connection to Missouri, other than being the place of my birth and where my ancestors were buried.

The service was, as I suspected it would be, solemn and respectful. My father's minister conducted the service and I was asked to present the eulogy. My and my father's friends and some distant relatives came and paid their respects.

As I boarded the plane in St. Louis to fly back to Alabama, the only sadness I felt was that I would probably never see my closest friends again. Some had become like brothers and sisters to me.

Chapter 14

Some time later, after I felt as if I had finally settled into my new position as pastor of the Rumble Creek Baptist Church in Rumble River, Alabama, I looked at the calendar and suddenly realized I had been pastor of a church for almost a year. I was happy and it appeared I was doing a good job, but then it happened.

I was so happy and involved in my church people and activities that I failed to pay close attention to the world around me. I knew the war in Vietnam had been brought to a close. The assassination of a president was sinking into history, the racial unrest in the state where I was living and in surrounding states had quieted down, and I thought there was nothing to worry about except what my sermon on the next Sunday would be.

I thought it was simply a carryover from the protests staged by the young people during the Vietnam War. However, it proved to be racial prejudice rearing its ugly head once more. A small black church, not too far from Rumble Creek, had been attacked and burned. It was done at night, so thankfully no one was hurt or killed, but the flames of racism began to burn brightly around my little piece of heaven on earth. My priority for human rights was immediately singed by the same flames, and I let it be known. Most of my congregation appeared to support my views, but a few either said nothing or let me know they felt I was on the wrong side.

My next sermon was a scorching condemnation of anyone who held the view that color of skin was an excuse to torture and torment a fellow human being. Some of my parishioners got up and walked out during my sermon, but most appeared to agree with my words. I tried to use the words the old priest had said to me in Vietnam, "God loves everyone, even the bad if they turn to doing good."

I hoped that I said things the way God meant them to be said rather than letting my anger say them in an ungodly way.

As we left the church after the service, Miss Effie asked me to come to her house for dinner. She seemed a little distraught, so I accepted her invitation, thinking perhaps we needed to talk.

Her southern fried chicken was superb, along with the crispy-crust apple pie. Then it was time to talk. Miss Effie asked me if I understood the South.

I asked in return, "What do you mean by 'Do I understand the South?'"

"Brother J. R., today you scalded some of your church people!"

"Yes, I realize I did. But my job is to teach the words and desires of God. And he does not want us to judge our fellow man by the color of his skin. He wants us to judge the size and outlook of his heart."

"Brother J. R.," she said, and then she stopped. "Brother J. R., what does the J. R. stand for?"

Before I could think, I told her, "James Riley."

"Then why not call yourself James Riley Cole?"

Slowly I told her my story. As I finished, she said something that I had not had the guts to admit.

"Brother James, I will keep your secret, but always remember almost all of us have something we would like to hide, and that is why some of the church members walked out. They also have things in their background they would rather keep secret, even though God knows what they are." Then she continued, "Brother James, you are a fine pastor and I am so happy that God placed you here with us, so would you prefer that I not divulge your secret at this time?"

Thinking quickly, I replied, "Could we keep this between the two of us until I can find a way to smooth out the wrinkles I have caused in my congregation?"

"What would you prefer to be called if the question ever arises, from others, concerning the J. R.?"

Then it hit me. "Perhaps you could say my name is Jeremiah Riley Cole."

She agreed to handle the situation in that way, and I thought perhaps I should have the big Colt close by if it were needed.

With that thought in mind, I decided I would keep the old revolver close in the parsonage and then place it under the towel I had on the lectern to wipe my face during the sermons on Sunday mornings. Having the old pistol in my thoughts, I realized I had been leaving it in the drawer of my desk in the parsonage office. Because of safety and security, I very quickly purchased a small bolt-down safe and installed it in one of the parsonage closets.

Chapter 15

More and more the feelings in the surrounding area and in the church remained supercharged. White members who had never appeared to be anti-black began to look for problems concerning the black members of the community.

I softened my language concerning the anti-black feelings but continued to press that God's message was to love each other, no matter the difference in skin color. Some of those who had walked out earlier seemed to accept my words and moved back into the church's activities, but a couple of families did not return. A little later I learned that one of the families had moved out of the community, but the other family, the Humphreys, continued to remain away from the services.

Little by little, I began to pick up bits and pieces of talk around the area, that the Humphrey grandfather had been involved in the hanging of a local black in the early part of the century, and the family had become fearful of reprisal after the civil rights movement began. Also one of the grandsons, Jerod, about my age, remembered me from Vietnam. It seemed he and I were somehow in the same place at the same time, and he knew of my reputation as a commanding officer. He convinced his family that the best thing they could do to defend themselves was to run me out of town, and the best way to scare me away was to burn down the church.

After giving the rumors a lot of thought I decided I would start sleeping in the church and keeping watch over the building at night, as all the misdeeds around the area were carried out in the dark.

I bought a number of baby monitors from stores outside our community and secretly placed the transmitters all around the outside of the church. I placed the receivers in the tiny room I used as an office and kept them hidden during the day. I also wore the old gun belt and carried the big Colt on my hip at night. Sometimes I felt that there was another person with me as I continued to guard the old church.

One night we had a chili supper in the basement of the church and it appeared everyone in attendance had a fantastic time of fellowship. After the meal, everything was cleaned up and the members slowly melted away to their homes and farms.

I walked to the parsonage and made preparations to return to my place of watch at the church. When I arrived, I reentered without turning on any lights. I always slept in some old clothing so that if anything happened I could slip on my shoes, grab the old Colt, and move out to defend God's house.

I was sleeping soundly on the old couch when one of the baby monitor receivers came to life. I could hear movement outside the east wall that was closest to the surrounding woods and underbrush. I stepped into my shoes, picked up the old gun belt, and strapped it around my waist. Quickly and quietly I hurried to the back door and slid out into the darkness behind the building. As I cautiously peered around the corner of the building, I could see in the glow of a streetlamp down the street someone between the woods and the building carrying a bucket. Before I had time to think, the old pistol was in my hand, and it took control of itself. I felt the recoil of one shot, but there was almost no sound of a report. Then I saw the bucket leap away from the figure and roll across the ground. At the same time I felt more than heard a voice scream, "Don't shoot again! Please don't shoot me. I don't want to die!"

Then I realized the figure was that of a child. With fear and remorse in my mind, I holstered the old weapon, rushed forward, and then smelled gasoline. As I got closer I also saw an unlit torch made of a stick and old rags. I once more drew the old revolver and continued toward the young man. When I finally covered the last few feet and came close to the child, I recognized him as the Humphrey's youngest son. He had his hands as far above his head as he could reach and he was crying. "I peed my pants!" He moaned, "Please don't shoot me. I'm sorry, I'm so sorry!"

In my gruffest voice I said, "If you're so sorry, why were you doing what you were doing or getting ready to do?"

Then he collapsed to the ground and began to wail, "I heard my daddy and my uncle talking about you and the church. My uncle said they needed to either scare you away or kill you, and he believed the way to scare you was to burn the church down. He said, and I'm sorry for the words, "Cole is a mean, tough son-of-a-bitch and he probably won't run, but will stand and fight—him and that old gun of his."

As the young man continued to tell his story, he stopped crying and became fairly calm. I was beginning to wonder why no one had come running when they heard the sound of the shot and young Humphrey crying. Then it hit me. There was no sound, and there was still none as we were talking. Then young Jamie, as I remembered his name, continued, "I knew my uncle and daddy would be in big trouble if they were to do what they planned, so I decided to bring a can of gas, a torch, and some matches and leave them close to the church like someone was planning to burn the church down. I figured then they would hear about it and decide the church would be guarded after that and give up on what they wanted to do. I only did it to stop my daddy from getting put in jail. My momma and us kids need him at home."

I thought for a time and then said, "Jamie, you get your little behind home and don't you say a word to anyone about this. If I hear anything about this I will have your daddy arrested. If I don't hear anything I'll not tell anyone and we will pretend it never happened. However, I may talk about the three things you brought, but not about you. Maybe your plan will work just the way you planned." As he got up from the ground he said, "Brother Jeremiah, thank you, and would you give me a hug?"

I shoved the old pistol back into the holster and hugged the young man as he quit shaking. Then when I released him from the hug, he turned and ran off into the darkness toward his home.

I stood there for a long time and thought back through all that had just transpired. Then I began to collect the evidence. When I started to pick up the gasoline container I was shocked by what I found. The one shot that the old gun fired—and it fired itself, because I knew I didn't even have my finger in the trigger guard— cut the wire bale of the gas can on both sides of the handle. Even I could not shoot that accurately, especially in the dark.

I worried about fingerprints on the old can, but I decided God would help me smooth that over if any smoothing was needed. At least I knew I might have an enemy out there in the uncle. That was valuable information.

Chapter 16

I was no sooner able to quench the fires of fear in the Humphrey family when another small flame erupted in, of all places, Effie's family. I was busy in my office at the church attempting to bring all the past problems together in a group so I could perhaps solve some, if not all at the same time. Effie rushed into my office and I knew by her demeanor she had a personal problem and was not able to use her years of experience to reach a solution.

"Effie, what's wrong? You look like a hive of bees are on your trail."

"It's my granddaughter Ellie. She's been in Chicago working since her divorce. The company she was working for has shut its doors and she has not been able to find employment. She's talking about trying to borrow money from a questionable loan firm until she can find a job. She has no family up there. I don't want her to put herself in debt without a positive way to pay back the loan. I've been trying to get her to come here and live with me until she is back on her feet. but she says 'How do I get back on my feet if I don't have a job down there?' And I don't have an answer to that question, so I'm afraid she will do something foolish and never be free from problems ever again."

One of the problems I was wrestling with before Effie came in was that our church custodian, Leo Harps, had just contacted me with the news his doctor ordered him to cease working because of a heart condition.

55

"Effie, would your granddaughter be willing to work as a custodian? The church will need one, because Harps has just resigned." As I explained the situation to Effie, another idea crossed my mind. I was getting tired of cleaning my parsonage and cooking my evening meal.

"Effie, I would also hire her to clean the parsonage and cook my evening meal, and she could eat that meal with me at no cost to her. Together the two wages should be enough to almost meet an average wage in Chicago. And she would also not be paying the high Chicago taxes. Oh, can she cook?"

A happy little smile began to spread across Effie's face as she answered, "Brother Jeremiah, thank you so much. I'll call her tonight and make the proposal. And yes, I believe she can cook." Then a dark shadow appeared in her eyes. "But she will be living in my house, not in the parsonage!"

I laughed as I answered, "No! Effie she would not be living in the parsonage with me. I've enough problems without that one."

Effie left my office in a much better mood than when she entered, and I was allowed to return to my problems. But perhaps one of them would be solved in a short time.

Almost before I was out of bed the next morning, Effie was on my phone accepting the job offer for her granddaughter. Then Effie explained that her granddaughter would move to Rumble River as soon as she could pack and do away with her unnecessary belongings.

In about two weeks Ellie appeared in my office to finish all the paperwork and get the instructions on what her job would require. She introduced herself as Ellie Mae Duren as she shook my hand. I was pleasantly surprised. She was a younger copy of what I had always pictured Effie to be as a young woman.

I had never been interested in a girl or woman before, other than in a friendly manner. However, Ellie caused me to catch my breath. Something caused me to feel a start and I didn't know what it was. Then I realized that she was explaining back to me what she understood the job to be.

56

"I will be responsible for cleaning the church, doing dusting, window washing, washing of any fabrics needed in or for service, and other small details. What about repairs of church equipment?"

"No. I will take care of the equipment or I will hire someone to do any needed repairs that I can't accomplish."

"Now what about the parsonage and your meals?" she asked.

"The job includes caring for the parsonage and you will only be required to prepare the evening meal. And you will be welcome to partake of the evening meal with me at no cost to you."

"Grandmother said at no time would I be required to sleep at the parsonage, that I would dwell in her house."

"That is absolutely correct. You will not be sleeping on the parsonage premises."

Then she said, "I believe I will be able to handle the job. Now what will be the wages?"

We discussed how much the church and I could pay for her services and she accepted the offer. As she left my office she turned and with a beautiful smile said, "I'll be back at the parsonage at four-thirty to start the preparation of our first meal. Do you have anything on hand or should I go shopping?"

I reached into my pocket and got out my keys to the parsonage and handed them to Ellie.

"Maybe you'd better check my pantry and see what you think. Then I took out my billfold and handed her five twenties and said, "Purchase whatever you might need for the next two or three meals, as I have a habit of eating junk most of the time."

Once more she turned to the door and disappeared from my sight. However, she did not disappear from my thoughts. For a few moments I found myself praying for forgiveness, as some of my thoughts of Ellie were not of the type that God would approve. However, even though I knew my thoughts were sinful, I couldn't keep them out of my mind as I thought of Ellie and how beautiful she was.

As time went on, my thoughts became more and more involved with her being in my life and I was also aware and worried about the difference in our ages. I believed there had to be a span of over ten years between us.

Chapter 17

The first meal Ellie served was just one more problem in my initial confrontation with boy meets girl. The food was so good and she was so pretty that I started having a real problem with—what, love? I didn't even know what it was and then I thought, "Am I in the very middle of a mess like that?" I made myself a promise. I would stay out of that woman's way as much as I could. But then a problem from the past came creeping back to the door of my church. Evidently Jerod Humphrey, my old acquaintance from Vietnam, remembered my name had been Captain James R. Cole and began to question why I was using the name Jeremiah in Rumble River. Shortly some of my parishioners also began to ask the same question. Then I quickly understood why God does not want us to lie. I decided the best way to defend myself was to tell the whole truth.

The next Sunday my sermon was on the sin of making false statements. I immediately admitted my name was actually James Riley Cole, and I continued to tell the whole story of my problems at home in Missouri and why I moved to Alabama.

Before any hard questioning started, Miss Effie informed the congregation that she already knew the facts but allowed me time to prove myself as a real minister before she would come forth and reveal the actual information.

59

Her statement quieted the major concerns, but one gentleman asked why I adopted the name Jeremiah. I explained that Jeremiah in the Bible was scared by God's command to speak what he was directed by God to say. And then God told Jeremiah he would protect him as he spoke. I also wanted God's protection as I started to be a minister when I really didn't know how. The old gentleman suggested I continue to be Brother Jeremiah as an honor to God and the first Jeremiah. I thanked him for his faith in God, Jeremiah's teaching, and me. The uneasiness passed and I was once more in good stead with my congregation.

Chapter 18

After the cleansing of my soul and conscience in front of almost all of my parishioners, I began to ease into a regular routine. Ellie was in my life every day. She cleaned, cooked, and slowly began to check my sermons, plus cue me on the correct etiquette for the actions of a church minister. In turn, I tried to assist her and Effie with any small, day-to-day problems they happened to encounter. They both made me feel very happy and helped ensure my success.

For an extended period of time I believed my life was finally settled and the only worries I had were doing the correct minister things and controlling the wild thoughts that I had developed concerning Ellie. I really didn't know but I supposed what I had developed was love. And I didn't know what to do about it.

But even that dilemma rapidly moved to the back burner as Jerod Humphrey moved back into full view. For whatever reason, I became his main target for ridicule and damnation. He appeared to be determined to destroy me and my life, and for what reason I had no explanation. So like the real Jeremiah, I decided to face him head-on to try to determine what our problem was. I watched around town until one day he appeared in front of Raymond Hope's store. I walked toward the store and calmly greeted Jerod with a simple, "Good morning, Jerod."

He turned toward me and his eyes bulged and suddenly his face turned almost a deep red. "Don't good morning me, you sinful bastard. You killed fifteen men and then you become a minister to escape punishment for the killings. I was there. I know all about it. You deserted your men and ran and they all paid the price!"

I calmly stated in return, "Jerod, I never ran. I was injured and out of action when my men were killed. I'm a minister today because my head injury forced me out of the army. I draw a disability pension because of that head injury. No one, not even you, mourn the deaths of those men more than I."

Jerod drew in a deep breath and almost screamed, "I'll see you dead, you black-hearted bastard! Someone has to make you pay, and I plan to be the one."

With that statement he turned and almost ran out of my presence. At that moment, or a little before, Jamie's father came out of the store and stepped in front of me. "Brother Jeremiah. First, I want to thank you for what you did for my son. Yes. I know he was not to tell me about it or I would go to jail. But Jamie is a good son and you are a good pastor. Jamie told me about the problem and I have been so ashamed that I even let my brother approach me with such a scheme. But now there is a bigger problem. Jerod is either drinking or drugging. I don't know which. But now he believes he is God's instrument to extract payment from you for your men's deaths. He said he would kill you and I'm afraid he will try. As hard as it is for me to say, don't let it happen. Kill him first, if you must. He has not been right since he returned from the war, but the war is to blame, not you."

As something swelled up in my throat, I replied, "Mr. Humphrey. It takes a mighty big man to admit he has been wrong, and you are a mighty big man, and I thank you for your wisdom. I plan to do all I can to keep Jerod from doing anything to destroy himself."

"Brother Jeremiah, I don't want to be a big man, only a good father."

We shook hands and parted, he to his home and me back to my office to try to figure out what to do about Jerod Humphrey.

Chapter 19

After the meeting with Jerod Humphrey I began to realize that I had two major problems. I had the love for a beautiful woman biting me from one side and the hate of a man biting me from the other. I knew I had to solve one or the other of the problems or I was going to be a basket case, like Jerod.

The first thing I decided I had to do was protect myself from a possible attack by Jerod. I thought he might make an attempt very soon. My love for Ellie would not kill me immediately, even though I was beginning to think it might in the not-too-distant future if I didn't do something. But I was so old, how could she feel anything for me?

For the present I decided I would start carrying the old Indian War's relic to protect myself if Jerod made an attempt on my life.

A couple of days later, Mr. Humphrey called and said Jerod had disappeared and that he left a note saying he was leaving the area for good before he did something stupid. I hoped that he would find help somewhere or somehow and would not make a stupid move.

Then it was back to thoughts of Ellie. I continued to work on my sermons and the like, and Ellie continued to clean and cook. But I began to notice that there was a frown on her face some of the time as if happiness was attempting to depart from her personality. I tried to make jokes and created humor when we were together, but she seemed to widen a gap in our friendship. Because I had not seen or heard anything from or about Jerod, I returned the old gun to its place in the little safe.

Then one day, perhaps several weeks or months later, Ellie came into my office and told me she was searching for other employment, preferably out of the community. I asked her if she needed more compensation for the work she was doing.

"No. I have just become unhappy here in Rumble River, living with my grandmother and not seeing the rest of the world."

I told her I understood and that I would help her find another job. I felt like the world was ending for me during our conversation.

Though I didn't sleep very much that night, I was determined to find a place for Ellie to work, where she would be happy. I loved her too much to not help her in any way I could.

Then a thought entered my mind. Perhaps Effie could shed some light on what type of job Ellie was looking for and where she wanted to go to find work. That way I could help her locate the exact type of employment she wanted to do. A conversation with Effie would be my next move.

When I arrived at Effie's home she was busy preparing some baked goods for a women's group sale the following day, and her house smelled like what I imagined heaven smelled like. As I began to question Effie about Ellie's desires she began to question me about how well Ellie was accomplishing her work for me. I told her that I couldn't have been happier with what Ellie had done. Then a small smile curled Effie's lips and she said, "How do you personally feel about Ellie?"

With a smile I answered, "I really like her a lot. She's a fantastic young woman and she does a great job cleaning and cooking."

"Is that all you feel about her?" Effie dug into my mind with a sharp tongue.

Almost in a whisper, I answered, "I think I love her! But she's so young, what would she see in me?"

"Have you told her? Oh, and have you asked her not to leave? Maybe you're just a middle-aged fool."

"Miss Effie. Do you think she could ever love me, and do you think she might stay, if I asked?"

"No one will ever know if you don't ask."

I don't remember if I said anything else to Miss Effie, but I do remember running back to the church to find Ellie.

She was, of all things, cleaning the main bathroom in the foyer of the church. I decided that I had faced Viet Cong bullets and lived through that, so I just charged ahead into perhaps pain worse than death—being rejected by the woman I loved.

"Ellie," I addressed her. "I don't know any other way to say what I'm going to say, so here goes. I love you and I don't want you to leave. You're so much younger than me, I know it's crazy, but I love you!"

"Only about ten years younger, and that doesn't matter to me."

Rushing on, I almost yelled, "I want to marry you and keep you here with me."

"Hey, Preach! You didn't hear we're only about ten years apart in age, and that doesn't bother me. And I love you too."

I don't know if I did it right, but at least I tried to kiss her. I knew I wasn't any good at it, but I sure intended to learn. That is, if she was willing to teach. I never found out how it happened, but within two days the whole state knew Ellie and I were a pair. Maybe not the whole state, but the whole crazy area around Rumble Creek knew the parson was probably going to take a wife. And who was the happiest one of all? The parson!

As quickly as I could get away from Ellie after I proposed—if what I did was a proposal—I hurried back to the church to get on my knees and thank God for such a wonderful gift.

For a few days Miss Effie was the most popular grandmother in Rumble Creek, and she ate it up. And I continued to be the happiest preacher!

Because I had no close relatives and Ellie never talked about any close ties in her family, we decided to be married as soon as we could make the necessary plans and arrangements. It appeared Effie and the church congregation would make up the total guest list for our wedding.

Strangely, I had made contact some time back with the old Catholic priest that had guided me on my way to becoming a minister. He was retired and living in Florida, so I called and asked him to perform our wedding ceremony. He answered that he was quite old, but if his grandnephew would drive him to Alabama he would join us in holy matrimony. His grandnephew drove and he tied Ellie and me together on June 16, 1985. The ceremony was solemn, Ellie was beautiful, and we became husband and wife on a grand, sunny, Alabama day.

The following day we moved Ellie's small amount of personal effects into the parsonage and started our new life as a married couple. I felt I was the happiest man on earth.

Chapter 20

For a few months I had nothing on my mind but my ministry and my beautiful wife. Ellie and I getting married so quickly after I proposed might seem odd, but we had almost been living together for a long time. We were together in my house or the church almost every minute of every day except to sleep, so we probably knew as much about each other as most married couples. We had just not hugged, kissed, or consummated the arrangement. I was such a fool I never realized what I had been missing, but I was determined to make up for lost time. Ellie never again mentioned leaving Rumble River or looking for a job someplace else. Ellie and I continued to live in the little parsonage and decided we would not leave unless I gave up my preaching position or we started a family. I didn't plan on leaving Rumble Creek and I decided Ellie and God would make the decision on a family.

The racial problems in the South appeared to become less and less talked about or acted upon and I was very pleased about that. It had also been a long time since my past had been mentioned around the area and I was extremely pleased about that. I had become Brother Jeremiah or simpler yet, Reverend Cole.

With all the goodness surrounding Ellie and me, the old family heirloom moved further and further from my mind. Once in a while I would remove it from the little safe to clean and admire it. It was still as beautiful and fully functional as the day it left the Colt factory. I couldn't understand how, after years of handling and military use, it was still as fine as when it was new. Each time I touched it I felt a warmth in it, not just cold hard steel. Sometimes I found myself talking to it as if it were another human being. But in all fairness, my grandfather, my father, and I all probably owe our lives to it, and a man never forgets a debt like that. When it was time to return it to the safe, I always felt a little sadness, as if I were placing one of my family in a dark prison cell away from the happiness of everyday life. But no matter what I believed, it was still only wood and steel.

As the days, weeks, and months carried us forward, Ellie and I became more and more acquainted with each other's likes and dislikes and our outlooks on life itself. We finally got around to a discussion of increasing our family. Of course we discussed our ages as a plus or minus to starting a family. Ellie quickly admitted she really would like to be the mother of at least one child. I had never really thought about being a father, as I had never contemplated ever being married. I had always believed I would be forever in the military and might be killed in some action in the world. The thought of fathering a child became a great thrill in my mind, but at the same time it raised a greater fear about being a success as a parent. We decided to leave it up to God to make the decision for us because no matter what eventually happened, He would always be our Lord and Master.

As in every man's life, there were good days and bad days, so we took them as they came.

Then one day I heard rumors that Jerod Humphrey had been seen back around Rumble River, although no one knew why he came back or what his thoughts were.

One morning just as I left the breakfast table and headed into the little room that was my office, there was a knock at the door. When I opened it Jerod Humphrey was looking in at me. Then I saw Jamie standing a little behind him. Jerod slowly raised his hands up in front of his face with his palms toward me and then he slowly spoke.

"Reverend Jeremiah, please forgive me. God has forgiven me and now I beg for your forgiveness."

Then I slowly answered. "Jerod, what do I have to forgive you for?"

"For being the devil's soldier and threatening your life. I'm badly hurt and I need everyone's help. And I need yours most of all. I want to be well, and I believe with God's and your help I can be. Will you sign papers as a retired United States Army officer saying I need mental treatment for problems caused by my service, so I can go into a military mental hospital for help?"

"Yes, Jerod. I'll sign papers and go with you to whatever medical facility you choose and personally witness to your needs."

As tears ran down his face, Jerod said, "Jamie said you would understand and help me if I asked, even after I accused you of not protecting your men. You're the brave one and I've become the damned drunk and druggie. Thank you, Brother Jeremiah."

I immediately made calls to some of the doctors who had treated me when I was injured and was able to get Jerod an interview. After a short time he was admitted to a facility not far from Rumble Creek at the NASA Space Center campus in Huntsville. A couple of months later we heard that Jerod was receiving treatment and making giant strides toward once more becoming a sane man. I went to the church and said a prayer of thanksgiving. Still later by a few months, Jerod was allowed to come home for a visit, and we could see he was becoming a brand-new man.

Chapter 21

Because of the mystery of the army Colt and its connection through my grandfather to the mythical General George Armstrong Custer, I researched every Custer fact or myth I could find, hoping to gain some information about my grandfather and/or the old Peacemaker. I read things Custer wrote about his career, articles he wrote for magazines, and I read about his interests and exploits, including his interest in various firearms he had accumulated during his career.

One late evening, while watching a local television channel that sometimes aired news oddities from around the nation I saw and heard a segment of a strange story from a northern newspaper. The article was written about an inspector who had worked for the Colt Company in the 1870s. The article stated that the old gentleman lived in a house near the Colt factory and had died there sometime after 1900. The home had changed hands several times over the years and eventually was purchased by the city of Hartford, Connecticut.

It was razed to build a city parking lot. Hidden somewhere in the old house was a box of papers belonging to the old firearms inspector. When the rotted structure came down, the box was found. It appeared that General Custer and the old man had been friends, as there were several letters signed by Custer and some news clippings telling of the June massacre in Dakota Territory in 1876. Then the article said there was also a

71

strange note from Custer in the papers. The note was a thank-you from Custer for the gift of a new army Colt revolver. Custer said he was very pleased by the gift and that the revolver was a fantastic firing weapon. Stranger still was a confession written by the inspector concerning the gift Colt. The old man wrote that during one of his inspections of a 150-piece order going to the US Army in 1875, he found one weapon to be faulty in a number of ways. His orders were to have any weapon with that many problems destroyed. However, he held the army Colt back and decided to try some ideas he had developed on the worthless weapon. Later, after some evening work at home at his kitchen table, he succeeded in making the pistol function. Still later, he decided since it was to be destroyed anyway, he would give it to his friend Custer while the general was in Washington facing inquiries in the early summer of 1876. The old man continued in his writing that Custer was very pleased with the gift and said it was a very accurate weapon. At the bottom of the note, the old man further explained that because it was actually a theft that he had committed, he decided after Custer's death to simply leave a note telling the story. Then after his death, if the old gun reappeared, history would know the story.

At that point I was wide awake, but the note did not tell the story as to why the old pistol appeared to react on its own when combat was imminent. After a little more thought, and as I began to yawn, I decided it was time to join Ellie in bed where I could think about the next day's work and perhaps get some sleep. But I remembered to return the old Colt to the little safe, along with some notes I had taken that pertained to the newspaper article.

For another length of time, my church duties, Ellie, and my household activities kept my mind away from anything concerning the old revolver. I always knew it was secure in the little closet safe, but sometimes memories of my war years and the military duties fulfilled by my father and grandfather would cause me to want to physically feel the old pistol in my hand and I would be forced to take it out of the safe and, like a child, play with it.

As I once more thought about my old friend from the little safe and the past newspaper article, I pondered the apparent manufacture date of the historic Colt. However, I was still disturbed by the mysterious aura that the old weapon seemed to possess.

After all I had been told by my father about its supposed ability to almost think on its own during moments of duress, and after what I had witnessed as I carried it in combat and later in civilian life, I began to question its abilities or my own sanity. Could I really believe in God and also believe in ghosts and goblins? What I was beginning to think scared my being and caused me to fear for my very soul. By some quirk, could the old relic be haunted by the ghost of a long-dead general? Was Custer using the Colt when he was killed and by some paranormal phenomenon trapped in the cold steel of the old army Colt?

The only thing I could think of was go to God in prayer, but how could I pray about something that strange? Immediately the answer became very clear. I simply asked God to lead me where he wanted me to go. I retrieved the old gun, gun belt, holster, and cartridge case from the small safe I had in the closet of the little parsonage and laid them out for God to see. Then I waited hopefully for some sign from God.

But as I waited for a possible sign from God, I couldn't resist touching the old Colt, the same way I would have placed my hand on the shoulder of a near, dear friend. I recalled the many times the strange weapon had been the difference between life and death. Suddenly the steel of the pistol seemed to emit warmth into my hand as I almost sensed the presence of another human being. Without thinking I began to address the old relic as if I were talking... to a living human. I said, "General, have you been trapped in this piece of steel these many years since 1876?"

Then I noticed that the cartridge case was open, and one dirty, tarnished, long Colt .45 round was lying on the table next to the belt. Once more the old weapon

73

fairly leaped into my hand for no apparent reason, as I felt myself reaching out to retrieve the single cartridge. Opening the loading gate, I fed the loose round into the empty cylinder of the Peacemaker. Then the butt of the big revolver nestled into the palm of my hand, and I felt the reassurance of an old and dear friend. In the deathly silence of the evening and being alone with my thoughts, I heard the click, click, click, click, click, as the deadly weapon advanced the cylinder until the tarnished round was directly beneath the hammer. Without any effort on my part, the barrel of the long Colt rose up in front of me and moved in an arc across the back wall of my little room. Suddenly I felt the recoil of the pistol but heard no sound of a firing report. Neither did I see or smell smoke from the muzzle of Custer's Colt. On the back wall of my little room I saw a black mark appear, but again I heard no thud of impact of a bullet hitting a solid surface. I realized what I was seeing looked like a small patch of written words, and the steel of the Colt was once more cool to the touch. I laid the old pistol on the table, stood up, and walked to the back wall to look at the small black spot. On the surface of the painted wall I saw what looked like handwriting. Looking closer I saw—written in a clear, black script—five words, "Take me to West Point!" To my amazement, the script then simply faded away.

I thought for a few moments and then I returned to the table and once more placed my hand on the butt of the 1875 Army Colt. The grip was once again warm to the touch. I asked, "You want me to place you in the museum at the Point?" The warm old relic again leaped into my hand and then quickly cooled until it felt like nothing more than the reverend's old Peacemaker.

"Old friend and protector, I will personally present you to the museum at West Point, and with the information we now have you will be recognized for what you were. And, General, a personal thanks to you—from my grandfather, my father, me, and my men—for your service in four US wars. We salute you."

74

Chapter 22

After the episode of the writing on the wall, I decided it was time for the old Peacemaker and the spirit of the general to finally be laid to rest in the military museum at West Point. Since Custer and his wife's graves are in the cemetery there, the spirit of the general should dwell there also.

The only problem I could imagine for the future was how I could present my plan to Ellie without it appearing to be an unusual action on my part.

One night after supper I casually mentioned to her that new information had come to light in Connecticut, and that my old family heirloom army Colt may have belonged to General George Armstrong Custer. And I believed if that was factual, the old relic should be put in the museum at West Point, so that every American could have the opportunity to see such an unusual historic treasure.

Immediately a strange expression appeared on Ellie's face. "So, General Custer's ghost is the wounded soldier that lives in this house with us?"

Then I'm sure it was my face that took on a weird expression. "What are you talking about?" I asked.

Ellie took a few seconds, I supposed to collect her thoughts. Then she began to speak, "You not appearing to be interested in me for anything but a housemaid before you finally said you loved me was only part of the reason I said I was going to leave. There was a second reason. One day as I was cleaning the bedroom, I turned quickly to go

75

get some cleaning supplies I needed, and there was the apparition of a badly wounded man standing behind me in front of the closet door. He looked to be about thirty-five years old with reddish golden hair. He was undressed except for wool long johns from his waist down, and part of a blue trouser leg with a gold stripe was wrapped around his ankle. He was bare-chested and covered with bloody wounds over almost all of his body. Before I could say anything, the image faded into nothingness and was gone. I was so mixed up at the time over you and me, I thought perhaps I was imagining things, so I just tried to forget it. But after we married and I moved in here, there was another occurrence. One night I woke up to use the bathroom and you were not in bed. I saw light in the kitchen, so I quietly walked in, thinking you were working on a sermon. You were sitting at the table with your hands clasped as if in prayer. Your chin was on your chest and your eyes were closed. Then I heard you speaking very softly. I really thought you were in prayer. I saw tears on your face and I heard what you were saying, but the voice wasn't yours.

"The voice said, 'General, I'm so sorry. If I had been there I know I could have helped. Reno's men told me later that even a hundred more men would have made no difference, only in the number of men killed. But I know I could have been of help. And if not, I could have at least died with you.'

"Then I saw him again. Only this time there was a horrible wound to the top of his head, as if it had been skinned like you would skin a possum or coon. Then as if he finally sensed I was there, he once more faded to nothing. From what you have told me about your family, I believe your grandfather was talking to General Custer through you."

"Why haven't you told me this before?"

"Because I was afraid you might think I was crazy, or that I might think you were crazy, because I suspected you might know things you were not telling me. And sometimes when you were handling the old pistol, you would slip and address it as General."

As we sat there I told Ellie the whole story, the parts she already knew and the parts she was unaware of. Then together we made plans for me to take the fantastic old piece of history to the Point.

First, I contacted the nearest VFW post and asked if they could contact the museum at West Point or get the telephone number of the curator of the museum.

In a few days they returned my call with the name and phone number of the curator. Early the next day I placed a call to the museum. I explained that I believed I had a firearm that had once belonged to General George Custer. The gentleman I contacted asked if it was from Custer's Civil War years. I told him it was a .45-caliber army Long Colt made in 1875, and I believed Custer was carrying it either on his person or in his saddle bags at the time of his death.

"Probably you are mistaken," he replied. "No weapon was reported picked up from the battlefield, especially one owned by the general."

Then I explained about my grandfather's service with the 7th cavalry before and after the massacre. I told how my grandfather came to have the army Colt and that he always claimed to have killed the war chief, Thunder Cloud. I also told him of the weapon being used by our family through three wars and during civil disturbances. Then I explained about the newspaper article from Hartford, Connecticut, and also gave him the serial number of the old piece. I further explained that I would be happy to keep the relic as a family heirloom—or give it to the museum. I finally concluded by suggesting he do the research about the gun to clear his own understanding and then contact me if the museum was interested.

In about a week I received a return telephone call from Curator Murry. After we exchanged greetings, he quickly informed me the museum did indeed desire to add the pistol to their holdings. He then asked what the price of the antique would be. I explained that a historic item of the old Colt's repute could not be priced, so it would be my family's and the general's gift to West Point as long as its full story would be told with the display.

He assured me that the whole story would be told and stated that their research almost definitely proved beyond doubt that the gun was Custer's. Their research revealed that a short time after the massacre, Thunder Cloud was never seen in any following combat, so the story my grandfather told of his death appeared to be true. The serial number was removed from the Colt records as being destroyed. The old inspector's and Custer's letters also appeared to prove the authenticity of the weapon, but perhaps the most convincing piece of paperwork in the museum's research was a piece I had not found. The Colt inspector, a man by the name of Buell, who gave the army Colt to Custer, had been a fellow graduate with Custer at the Point in 1861. Cadets Buell and Custer had been good friends and fellow drinking buddies at Benny Havens, a tavern about a mile down the hill from West Point.

Deep in my being I knew the true story that the curator didn't know, but I also knew the general deserved to go home to join his wife in eternal rest. As I prepared to hang up the phone, I asked, "If new information on the old pistol comes to light, even after it becomes the property of West Point, would you keep me informed?" He assured me he would.

As I hung up the phone, I knew I had done what was Christian and humane.

Chapter 23

Immediately after my phone conversation with Mr. Murry, Ellie and I discussed the delivery of the old gun to West Point. We talked of me flying to New York state while she stayed at home and took care of the church. I suggested we might drive up the Eastern Seaboard together on a much-belated honeymoon and vacation.

After more discussion and consideration we decided a leisurely auto trip would prove to be very enjoyable and we deserved it.

I placed another phone call to the West Point Museum and informed Mr. Murry we would hand deliver the historic artifact to the academy on the anniversary of the Battle of the Little Bighorn. He answered with an invitation to be the guests of the academy, stay in one of their dignitary accommodations, and be the guests of honor at a banquet commemorating the presentation of the Custer Colt to the museum. I accepted the invitations and thanked him for the consideration. Then it was time for Ellie and me to solidify our plans.

The first item on our agenda was to inform the church operations committee that I would be taking a long overdue vacation from my church duties to deliver a gift to the military museum at West Point. Some of my closest associates already knew the story of the old Peacemaker, but some of the members did not. So I once more told the story of the old weapon and how it had been a family heirloom since the Indian Wars in the west in the 1870s and how three generations of Coles had carried it in combat.

The part they had not known was that the old army Colt had belonged to General George Armstrong Custer and that he was carrying it at the Battle of the Little Bighorn.

I explained that Ellie and I were to be the guests of the academy to present the artifact to the museum. Everyone seemed to be extremely excited about that. I also told them that Ellie and I would start shopping for a newer car to drive to New York as I was afraid our old clunker wouldn't get us there and back.

Honest John Hart, the area used-car salesman, quickly spoke up and said, "Brother Jeremiah, I have an almost new 28-foot Chevy Recreation Vehicle that I keep to rent to vacationers. It would be my pleasure to loan it to you for your trip and save you the cost of a newer vehicle. However, if you are bent on making a purchase I would certainly be pleased if you came to my lot first."

One of the others in the group jokingly spoke up and said, "Brother Jeremiah, take the loan. Don't fill his coffers with your money for one of his junkers."

I thanked him for the offer and said I would run it by Ellie and we would get back to him. We shook hands and he said, "Brother Jeremiah, I'm really excited and pleased for you and Ellie to be recognized for your gift to the academy."

Then I said, "John, and I'm very happy and pleased to claim you and your family as great friends and members of my congregation."

That evening I told Ellie all that had happened at the meeting and we discussed the loan of the RV. Then she asked, "Jim, can you drive a rig like that?" I told her John had said it was no harder than driving a large pickup truck and I would test-drive it before we made any agreement.

Later, after test-driving the rig and talking more about it with John, we decided to give it a try.

As the days and weeks passed by I continued to remember all that the old army Colt had been to my family and all the lives the general had saved while it was firmly held in my grandfather's hand, my father's hand, and in my hand. History had sometimes in the past depicted Custer as less than a great commander, but I could view him as no less than a great friend and protector. I hated to part with the old firearm, but I knew it was time for it to become no more than a historic oddity and for Custer's spirit to be set free.

Chapter 24

Finally the day came for Ellie and me to leave Rumble Creek and head north to the Point. We had loaded the RV with food, drink, and the clothes we believed we would need for our great adventure. The general had a very special, secure spot in a storage box directly under the bed in the back of the unit. Of course all the women of the church each cooked a special dish and these were tightly packed in the travel vehicle's refrigerator. As we climbed into the cab, we were handed an envelope with best wishes from the entire congregation. As we motored out of town, Ellie opened the envelope and found ten fifty-dollar bills along with a note that simply said, "Have fun, newlyweds."

"What a fantastic congregation!"

During our planning time we had marked maps to follow that would lead us to the military academy. We also had a book to tell us where RV camps were located along our route. We had studied an atlas and knew we wanted to travel through Chattanooga and Knoxville, Tennessee; Roanoke, Virginia.; Harrisburg, Pennsylvania; and then to the outskirts of New York City. After that, West Point was only about fifty miles up the Hudson River. We decided to make no special plans to look for, or stop at any tourist sites along the way. We would simply enjoy whatever we came upon in route.

After a couple of hours on the road, we felt as if traveling was nothing out of the ordinary, as we were filled with happiness and fun. Ellie relaxed and began to look so much younger than her age.

The first surprise we encountered was the small low mountains we drove through from Chattanooga to Knoxville. There are hills in Alabama, but the hills in Tennessee were actually small mountains. Then we went through Roanoke and came in contact with remains from our nation's colonial period. Seeing Harrisburg revealed to us there were actually big cities in the farmlands of Pennsylvania. And then we saw New York City in the distance and realized just how small Rumble River really was.

After what amounted to a very leisurely five-day drive we pulled into the vicinity of West Point, just about an hour north of New York City. Looking in our camp book we soon located a spot where we could park the RV and then rent a small car to drive around the area. Ellie was all eyes as history was of great interest to her. West Point is so steeped in history that she could hardly catch her breath. And to be honest, being almost a career military man myself, I was also almost breathless to be there.

As soon as we were settled in, I placed a call to Colonel Murry. A short time back I had learned the curator of the museum was not a Mr., but a full bird colonel. Being past military, the first time I spoke with him, I should have realized he was a US Army officer.

Colonel Murry immediately invited Ellie and me to come to his office as he was extremely excited and wanted to see the general in person as soon as possible.

I told him as soon as we could rent a car and find our way to his office, we would be on our way. His reply to that statement was, "Do not rent a car! Is there a phone there that you can use to make a local call?" Then he laughed, "I guess there must be because you are talking to me on the phone right now." I assured him I could call at almost any time. With another laugh he dictated a number for me to call when Ellie and I were ready to come to his office, and then he continued, "While you are at the Point, you will have a car and driver assigned to you and your wife. For any transportation just call the number and you will be picked up within minutes. And as soon as we meet I will make arrangements for you to move into the dignitary housing for the rest of the time you are here." Then he continued, "I'm so thrilled about you having a Custer relic and donating it to our museum, I can hardly keep my thoughts straight. Hurry and bring it to me so I can see it, as it's all I can do to wait to hold it in my hand."

When our conversation ended and I hung up the phone, in my mind I knew exactly how he was feeling, and he did not, and would never, know the whole story.

As Ellie and I freshened up to meet Colonel Murry, I thought perhaps I should also freshen up the general. When the colonel would meet the general, I wanted the old weapon to be brightly spit and polished and at its finest. As I retrieved the quilted, clamshell pistol case from under the bed in the RV, I could visualize the brown shine of the metal and the polished wooden grips, and I knew the general would be standing tall.

I sat down at the table in the RV and slowly unzipped the clamshell case. When I folded the upper half of the quilted case back, I couldn't believe what I was looking at. The surface of the metal was no longer shiny brown. It had a dark patina and there were several nicks and abrasions in and on the metal. Neither were the wooden grips still beautifully polished. They also showed nicks and chips from much handling and wear. I grabbed the piece and looked at the serial number to see if someone had switched another old gun for the general. The serial number was correct. Then a little voice in my brain said, *Custer is finally home at the Point. He is at peace in his grave beside his beloved Libby. His spirit is finally free from the cold steel he has been forced to dwell in for so many years. When his spirit left it, the Colt no longer carried Custer's youth, so it aged accordingly.* Tears came to my eyes, as I said a prayer of thanksgiving to God.

I held the old relic in my hands for a few more minutes and then I took a soft cloth and wiped away any dust that might have settled on the general as we traveled from home. I moved my hand to return the pistol to the quilted case and then I saw it, a shiny golden disc about the diameter of a US silver half-dollar. But this item was gold. I picked the piece of metal out of the quilted case and gave it a closer examination. Then I realized what I was looking at. It was a high-quality Carson City twenty-dollar gold coin dated 1876. I could not imagine where it came from. It was not in the case when I put the general in it at home.

Just then my eyes were drawn to the manufacturer's tag that was sewn into the seam of the quilted case that stated the maker's name. The maker's name had disappeared and in its place was a short message written in the same ink script that had appeared on my wall at home. I looked closely and the script said, "This is a gift for your son." And the script was signed G.A.C. I quickly looked a second time, and as my mind became satisfied with what it said, it faded from view and was once more replaced by the gun-case maker's logo. That was exactly what the script on the wall at home had done, simply faded away. But I didn't understand, I had no son and it appeared Ellie and I would have no children. So what did the message mean?

Because the car was due at any moment to take us to the academy, I decided to put the coin away and talk to Ellie about it later. I wrapped the gold piece in a cotton handkerchief and put it in my briefcase for safekeeping and then put the briefcase in the box under the bed. As I picked up the clamshell case containing the old army Colt to deliver to Colonel Murry, the car arrived to pick us up.

The ride to the museum was both enjoyable and at the same time a little sad. I knew the general was gone from the old relic, and at the same time I also knew that the old relic would soon be gone from me. But I continued to give thanks to God for allowing me to have such a friend for so long in my life. I was also thankful that from now on it would belong to all Americans, not just to my family.

As we walked into the museum Colonel Murry was waiting at the door and escorted Ellie and me to his office where he would get his first look at the old general.

Chapter 25

As we preceded the colonel into his office a feeling of *déjà vu* came over me. Every military office looked the same, and the smell of woolen uniforms, tobacco, and old papers hung in the room like a cloud on a rainy, dreary afternoon. I felt as if I was once more back in Vietnam.

Ellie was fascinated by the pictures and war mementos decorating the walls and the ends of bookshelves. There were military metals in small cases, uniform parts, and weapons from far back in history and up to the present era. I was once more impressed with the military decorum that fairly oozed from the walls and all the surrounding furniture.

I placed the quilted gun case on Colonel Murry's desk as he invited Ellie and me to be seated in the two cushioned armchairs in front of him. After we were all seated, the colonel reverently unzipped the case, folded the top half back, and for a long moment simply appeared to worship the old relic with his eyes. Then he very gently picked the historic weapon up and examined it with the eye of a true student of military history opening the loading gate to check that the cylinder was empty, looking at every chip and scratch, hefting it to verify its weight, and then mouthing the serial number as he read it from the frame. At last, I heard him exhale the breath he had held back for several long seconds.

Almost in a whisper, he spoke, "What a beautiful piece! And to know it was once held and fired by the boy general. And even more to appreciate the fact he may have been holding it at the moment of his death."

And then, like a child with his first toy pistol, the colonel turned his swivel desk chair around and faced the back wall of his office. Raising the Custer Colt in his right hand, he pointed the muzzle at the right-hand corner of the room above the top window line and slowly moved the old Colt across the wall in the left-hand direction. At equal intervals he raised the muzzle as if the old pistol was firing. Suddenly I heard the sound of the hammer being drawn back and the tumbler and sear click. I thought surely the colonel is not going to dry fire the old weapon and perhaps damage the mechanism, but then I saw the hammer had not been moved. I sensed more than saw the old gun recoil in the colonel's hand, but strangely Murry did not seem to feel the recoil. On the wall where there would have been a point of impact if a bullet had been fired, there appeared a fine colored picture about the size of a small television screen of a young American Indian war chief standing in the light of a fire holding a skinning knife above his head. The first picture faded and a second scene appeared. The young chief had a wound to his head and was falling backward.

Then I sensed a second recoil, and at the point of impact, another picture. This time a large man in a long gray woolen coat and wearing a military helmet was standing in a dark opening holding a trench knife above his head. This time the large man was falling backward into the darkness. That picture also faded.

The third time the old pistol appeared to recoil, another picture appeared and I almost screamed. There, lying in the weeds and foliage of a jungle floor was a young man with a terrible head wound. I knew immediately it was me I was looking at. That picture faded and another appeared. The young man was still lying in the weeds, but over his body was a haze. On the edge of the haze was the old army Colt appearing to float in the air, and it was firing at something out of the picture. Once more there was a fade to black and another appeared. There were bodies in piles about ten yards out from where I was lying. Then it hit me, and I know I moaned, as Ellie touched my arm and asked what was wrong. I told her I must have dozed and then suddenly awakened. I realized she and the colonel did not see the movie I had been watching, but I believed the last scene showed that George Armstrong Custer's spirit had saved my life in that stinking jungle in Vietnam. Silently I said a small prayer of thanksgiving for Custer having lived and for my own life that he saved.

The colonel swung his chair back around to the desk and placed the Long Colt back in the quilted case. Then looking at Ellie and me he said, "Captain, this fine relic will, I'm fairly certain, become the centerpiece of our museum's entire military collection. You will be thanked officially at the banquet, but I want to personally thank you for such a gift now. He stood, reached across the desk to shake my hand, and for a moment my eyes flickered upward to the wall above the windows as one more picture appeared There mounted on his favorite horse, clad in his full dress cavalry uniform with the plumed helmet, and yes, though it was out of strict dress uniform, he was wearing the old holster and carrying the weapon that lay on the desk in front of me. But before the picture faded, I saw the general raise his hand and snap a salute in my direction. And I, with the greatest of military courtesy rapidly rose to my feet and returned the high military honor. Colonel Murry, seeing my action, immediately drew his hand back and with a huge smile returned my salute, believing my salute of honor was directed at him.

Though I was able to hide my feelings and the questions that the small movie brought to my mind, I knew that as soon as possible I had to have some answers. I understood the picture of the young war chief, as it was about my grandfather. I also knew that the man in gray was the German my father faced, and I understood that I

91

was the soldier with the severe head wound. But I needed to know about the spirit saving my life. As things stood at that moment I knew I would have to wait until all of the formalities at the Point were completed before I could do the research.

As all of those thoughts were churning in my mind I became aware that the colonel was speaking to Ellie and me, as he said, "Now it's time for me to get you settled into the dignitary housing for your visit here at West Point. As soon as I put the Colt in the safe, I will escort you to your complimentary quarters."

Chapter 26

Accompanied by the colonel, Ellie and I were driven back to the RV park to pick up our luggage and personal effects. I also retrieved the belt, holster, and cartridge case from the box under the bed and gave them to the colonel. Then the driver delivered us to the dignitary housing. I didn't know what to expect, but what we walked into I definitely didn't anticipate! The house was small but very dignified. It was of the quality of a five- or six-star motel. It had two bedrooms and would have fit into any high-class neighborhood in the United States. On site was a full-time maid and a cook, or perhaps I should say a chef. There was also a garage for the car and housing for the maid, cook, and driver.

After showing us through the accommodations, the colonel asked if there was anything else we thought we might need during our stay. I assured him we were very satisfied with what was offered. With a firm handshake he got back into the car to return to the museum. Ellie and I excused ourselves and napped.

After a while I awoke from my nap and saw that Ellie was still sound asleep. Being a little curious about the surroundings, I wandered outside the cottage for a short walk close by. Before I could leave the yard, I discovered a nice patio with furniture in the shade of a grape arbor. I decided to not walk, and just sat down in an easy chair to think.

The gold coin weighed heavy on my mind, but the Vietnam jungle movie weighed heavier. I thought I understood what the movie was saying, but I wasn't absolutely sure. Then another thought crossed my mind. I never saw the whole report on the action when I was wounded. I had access to parts of the report, but not all. I wondered if I could in some way gain access to all of the report. Then the light came on in my brain. I wondered if Colonel Murry might know how to access the entire report for me. I knew it was very selfish and would not be to God's liking to use the general as a lever to get the full report, but I decided to sin to find out. "Please forgive me, God, for what I plan to do."

I decided the next time I saw the colonel I would ask. With that thought settled, I began to think about the other question. What did the message mean, "This is a gift for your son." What did Custer's spirit know that Ellie and I didn't?

I decided I would discuss the movie and the coin with Ellie as quickly as I could. That thought had just cleared my mind when Ellie came walking in under the grapevines that grew over the patio furniture. "What have you been doing?" she asked. I started to say "thinking," but that didn't fill the gap I needed to fill. "We need to talk," I answered. After the usual, "What about" and so forth, I was able to start my explanation.

First, I told her about finding the gold coin in the gun case. She was as surprised and curious as I about that. But when I told her about the note saying it was a gift for my son, she was flabbergasted. Then she asked the most innocent question that almost knocked me over. "Have you been married before and have a son you haven't told me about?" Before I could hold my tongue, I blurted, "Hell no, Ellie!" Then guilt ran through me like a knife. "Forgive me, God," and then I continued, "Ellie, I'm sorry I said those words to you. But no, I'm as confused about the message as you. Maybe the general was making some kind of a joke. Maybe he will make it clear in the future."

"But the general is gone," Ellie said.

Not completely, I thought. *At least not yet.* Then I told her about the movies in Colonel Murry's office. I also explained that I did not know about the dead Viet Cong soldiers around me when I was wounded, and I definitely did not know that Custer's spirit had saved my life. Finally I told her of my plan to ask Colonel Murry to help me get the full report on my final combat action to see if an explanation could be found there.

She decided what I was going to do was probably sinful, but she would likely do the same thing if she were in my shoes.

Just as we were finishing our little discussion, the maid appeared and said there was a small mid-afternoon lunch at the dining bar in the kitchen. But it was not a small lunch. It was a superb meal. I realized by the time Ellie and I decided to leave DC, we would both be many pounds heavier.

Chapter 27

The next day Ellie and I started taking massive advantage of our car and driver. We spent a few days taking in as many of the tourist attractions as we could.

Of course, our first point of interest was the burial of the boy general and his lady.

As I stood near the graves, I could almost feel the presence of Custer standing next to me clothed in his full cavalry dress uniform. After all that had happened previously, I could not, as a past officer of the Army of the United States, depart the graves without rendering proper military honors. Though I was not in uniform, I still felt the need to give a proper salute to the military figure that I greatly respected.

Next we toured the West Point Museum, seeing many of the historical artifacts pertaining to the US Army.

On one tour our driver heard Ellie mention to me that she would love to visit DC or at least make a brief stop on our way home to be able to say she had seen Washington. Boldly butting in he said, "If you would forego one of your days at the Point, I believe I could secure a long one-day tour of the great city for you, and I could be your guide. We would 'chopper' from here to the city, spend the day, and fly back at dusk."

Ellie happily nodded, and the driver made the arrangements in just a couple of minutes using the radio in the car.

97

The next morning we arose early and were in the nation's capital before nine o'clock.

The Smithsonian was the first big one, until Ellie and I realized we could stay a month and still not see all of that institution.

We toured the FBI building and went in the Pentagon to see as much as they would allow us to see. As past military, I had to see that, and I was able to ask the colonel for help getting the records I wanted. He sent us to an office in the big five-sided building to see a friend of his. The file would be forthcoming, either before we left the Point or it would be sent to our house in Rumble Creek. Perhaps, then, I might learn more about my final battle from the complete records.

The early evening helicopter flight back to the Point caused me to relive some moments from my time in Vietnam. For Ellie it was one of the great moments of her lifetime, as she had never flown in a whirlybird before.

After almost a full week of being tourists, the day arrived for us to appear as guests at the West Point Museum to make the presentation of the old relic. June 25th was a beautiful day at the Point, and the sun shone bright and full all day. Ellie was finally a little fatigued after five or six days of constant touring. I was tired too, but I was still enjoying every moment of our trip, and the food continued to be tasty and fattening.

The presentation was very nice and extremely formal. Ellie and I had been measured and fitted for rented formal wear, so that everything would be in the Washington style. I thought it was a bit much, but I went along for Ellie's sake. The attendance was small but made up of very high-level personnel in the military history field. I knew that George Custer would have been an accepted equal to any or all of them.

I was told that another public reception would be held later when the entire display was completed, showing the general—the old Colt—at its very best.

At the presentation we attended, the army Colt was displayed against a backdrop of three of the most recognized pictures of Custer. The first was his graduation from the Point. Second was the photo of him and General Pleasonton on horseback at Falmouth, Virginia, during the American Civil War. The last photo, which was taken at a studio in New York in March of 1876, shows him standing in full dress uniform in front of a low wall with his plumed helmet on the wall at his side. That photograph was probably one of the last professional photographs of him taken before the Battle of Little Bighorn.

Not being a public speaker *per se*, only a backwoods preacher, I didn't speak for very long. I only conveyed our family's pride in being the caretakers of such a fine historic item for about a hundred years and how it served three generations of soldiers as a trusted and reliable sidearm.

As I finished my speech, I heard the faint strains of "Garry Owen" playing in the distance, perhaps only privileged to my ears. I knew the spirit of the general was there once more, riding ahead of the 7th into their destiny.

After much drinking of champagne and discussion of Custer and all his glory, despite his foolishness and shortcomings, the event came to an end. I was glad it was over, as I knew the young general they were talking about was not the same Custer I had come to know, respect, and depend on. At evening's end, Ellie and I expressed our thanks and said our goodbyes to all the new acquaintances we had made. We arranged to pay our camping bill the next morning so we could head back south. We spent our last night in the RV to enable us to make an early departure the next morning.

We had a few places we wanted to visit as we drove the byways back to Rumble Creek.

We decided to visit Richmond to discover the birth of the confederacy, then headed west to Lexington to pay homage to two great southern generals, Lee and Jackson.

There we experienced the Virginia Military Academy, where General Jackson taught, and the cemetery where he is buried. We also viewed General Lee's tomb at Washington and Lee University, where he was president after the Civil War. Next we traveled down the Blue Ridge Parkway to Asheville, then further south to Atlanta to investigate Sherman's raid to the sea. From there it was on into Birmingham and after another short drive, we arrived at home. The general was finally home and so were we.

When we pulled into Rumble Creek, though it was after dark, a welcoming committee was waiting in our front yard. Most of the church members were present to greet us and give hugs.

As we prepared for bed, I saw that Ellie's face had taken on an almost green color, and she said she was not feeling at all well. I asked if we should see the doctor immediately, but she said she was not that ill.

By morning she was! I heard her in the bathroom upchucking every bit of all she could release. I quickly called Dr. Backster. He had become Ellie's and my family doctor after I met him at the little free clinic that he administered just down the block from the parsonage. His family had left him bushels of money, and he decided to use it to help the sick. Like the church, he accepted donations but did not charge a fee. When he answered my call and I told him what the problem was, he said not to leave the house, as he would simply come by. And if Ellie's illness was serious enough, he would have her transferred to the hospital.

Almost before I hung up the phone, Dr. Backster was at the door.

As I moved some things around that we had taken out of the RV the night before, the doctor went into the bedroom and began to discuss Ellie's symptoms and perform an examination.

Suddenly Ellie let out a screech, "No!" And the doctor hollered for me to come into the bedroom.

He didn't have to call me. When Ellie screamed no, I was already headed for our room.

The doctor did not seem to be alarmed and Ellie had a smile from ear to ear. Ellie turned to me as I entered the room and said, "We have to move out of this house."

Suddenly, I felt fear. Had the ghost reappeared and scared her. What would the doctor think or believe? But because she was smiling, I also had to believe there was a different reason she said we had to move so I asked why.

"Because there's no room for a nursery," Ellie answered.

"What?" I said.

"You're going to be a father, Preacher." Ellie giggled and roared at her little joke, and as if to end a sick joke, I said, "When?"

Dr. Backster answered, "I would say in about seven or seven and a half months."

And then in my mind, and to myself, I said, *and it will be a boy, if I can believe a certain ghost.* But out loud, to Ellie and the doctor, I said, "What a blessing God has seen fit to bestow upon us."

Dr. Backster told Ellie to come to the clinic as soon as she felt up to it and they would do a total examination to determine if his conclusion was correct, and if it was, to start getting prepared for a new arrival.

A few days later she did, and his diagnosis was correct. I was happy beyond anything else I had ever experienced.

I hurried to the church, knelt at the altar, and gave thanks to God. And then I also thanked a certain ghost.

Chapter 28

No matter what else transpired, I still had to work, and preaching was my calling and occupation. With that in mind I got my briefcase out of the closet where I had placed it when I took it out of the RV. As I placed the case on my desk and opened it, I saw the balled-up cotton handkerchief and remembered the gold coin. How had I forgotten about the gold coin? I supposed the jolt I received about becoming a dad had burned my brain a little. As I lifted the handkerchief out of the case, it felt bulkier and heavier than when I hid the gold coin in it. As I unfolded and spread out the handkerchief, not one but four gold disks rolled out and settled on my desk. I recognized the one I found earlier that predicted I had a son. But the other three I had not seen before. One of the three matched the first one perfectly. One of the last two was a ten-dollar gold coin with the date of 1842, but the last one was strange to me. I felt it had to be a Spanish coin of some type. As a child I heard stories and saw movies about Spanish treasures. What the last one was I didn't know, but the bigger mystery was what the last three coins meant.

I picked them all up and went to find Ellie. She knew the story of the first one but had still not seen it. Now there were three more coins, and one big mystery.

As I caught up with Ellie she was making the bed and straightening up the bedroom.

103

First, I showed her the coin from the gun case. She giggled and said, "So that's the coin that is for our son? You really believe the baby is going to be a boy, don't you?"

"Yes," I said.

"Ellie giggled and said, "We'll see."

As my thoughts continued, I told myself if Ellie did not object, I intended to honor the general and my grandfather by naming our first son George Samuel Cole.

Then I showed her the second coin that was like the first and explained where I found it. She appeared to be stunned. "Why a second one?" she asked. I shook my head as I showed her the other two. She touched the ten-dollar coin and said, "Why a smaller coin and an earlier date?"

Then a spark ignited my brain. "1842—I believe that was Libby Bacon Custer's birth year. She's a girl and smaller. Could that coin mean a girl child for us?"

Ellie immediately chimed in, "And the second coin like the first means a second son. Do you think we will have two boys and a girl?" she asked.

I shook my head a second time and said, "I don't know."

Then we both looked at the fourth coin. Ellie said it was an old Spanish gold piece because she had seen some in a museum in Chicago a few years earlier and they were very rare and expensive, but both of us wondered what that coin meant.

Ellie said, "No matter what any of them mean, you put them in a safety deposit box in the bank. They have to be worth a lot of money."

I never even paused. I wrapped them back in the handkerchief, put them in my pocket, and went straight to the bank.

I rushed home from the bank as quickly as I could to tell Ellie what I had learned. She stopped the chore she was working on to listen to what I had to say. I told her as I was filling out the paperwork for the safety deposit box, Jack Combs, the bank president, came walking by and asked why I needed a safety box. I laughed and told him

I had found an old coin and decided it might be valuable enough to keep in a bank box. He said he collected a few coins and could probably tell me the value of anything I might have found. Something or someone whispered in my ear, "Only allow him to see the one coin." We went into his office and I showed him only the Spanish piece. For a few moments he seemed unable to speak, and then he said, "Brother Jeremiah, the coin you have is one of only a small number of that type. The value, I believe, would be in the neighborhood of seventy or eighty thousand dollars."

We both rushed out to put the coin in the box. As I turned to put the box back into its security slot, I slipped the other three coins inside also.

Then I looked Ellie in the eye and said, "I believe that one coin will be enough collateral to allow us to borrow money to buy a house if we decide to or need to."

An odd look came over Ellie's face. "Is this really a gift from a ghost, and if so, why?"

Then both Ellie and I heard what sounded like the wind blowing through a narrow crack in the wall. "You took me home."

I saw Ellie drop her head as tears appeared in her eyes, and then she barely whispered, "God bless you, General."

Chapter 29

A short time after our arrival home from the Point, I received a yellow card from the post office. The card said I had a package that had to be signed for before delivery could be made. For a few moments I wondered what fancy letter or package was being delivered to me. Then I remembered the request I had made to Colonel Murry concerning the report on my last combat detail. Because of all the other excitement about a new baby and the gold coins, I had forgotten all about the report. I immediately left the house and walked directly to the post office.

The package was from the Department of the Army and was addressed to Captain James Riley Cole, Retired. I hurried back home as fast as I could walk, went directly to my little office room, and tore open the heavy envelope.

I immediately saw typed and handwritten pages. Some of the pages were freshly typed and some were xerox copies of originals. There were also maps. Some were copied from what looked like book pages and some were hand-drawn. I first started reading the newly typed pages. As I suspected, they were explanations for all the other pages in the big file.

Everything was just as I had been told by the two officers who took my report at the hospital, so I thought there was nothing else for me to learn. Then I looked closely at one of the hand-drawn maps and there was a paragraph or two written in longhand down in the right-hand corner.

107

They said, "When I found the captain he was still alive so I radioed the chopper above to send down a basket so he could be taken out. As I waited for the litter to be lowered I prepared the captain to be lifted out. His backpack was lying on his abdomen and he had one hand inside. As I removed his hand from the pack, he was gripping a big antique Colt revolver. Because I was afraid of some type of booby trap, I checked for wires and also checked the cylinder and found it was empty. I returned the old gun to the backpack and tied it to the captain's rifle, so it would go with him back to base. After he was evacuated, I surveyed the surrounding terrain. There I discovered a number of enemy soldier's bodies arrayed around the spot where the captain was lying, so I decided to see how they were killed. I assumed the chopper's gunners had kept them away from the captain. But what I found I cannot explain. Each of the dead, about ten in number, had one bullet wound to the forehead. Each wound was a kill shot. And every shot was from a large-caliber weapon, either a .45- or .50-caliber slug. If any chopper gunner can fire that accurately and consistently, I would like to congratulate him. But I have no other explanation."

Then I understood the little movie clip I saw above the window in Colonel Murry's office. The general was defending me as I lay wounded on the battlefield. I also knew then why the combined enemy force dissolved and disappeared. They were scared into total submission by the spirit haze that was defending my wounded body.

I bowed my head, closed my eyes, and begged God to guide and protect the soul of the boy general, our family's greatest friend.

As I finished my prayer Ellie came into the office and asked what I was reading, so I asked her to sit down as I told her the whole story. When I finished my tale, she looked puzzled for a few moments and then she asked, "Jim, do you think Custer's soul can ever be free from that old gun?"

Then it was my turn to become thoughtful. "Ellie, I don't know. I just assumed that when we got to the Point he would be free from the spell, the phenomenon, or whatever. But I never thought his horror could be for all eternity."

Once that thought entered my mind, I became a different man. I had a real problem, one that only God could solve.

Chapter 30

One morning as I was busy at my little desk preparing my sermon for the following Sunday's worship service, my phone rang. I was a little bothered by the interruption to my thought process, but I was very cordial as I said hello.

"Captain Cole is that you?"

I started to say, "That's who you were calling, wasn't it?" But instead I replied, "Pastor, Captain Cole, speaking."

"I'm sorry. I will always remember you as Captain James R. Cole, United States Army. This is Colonel Murry at West Point, and I have a surprise for you and your wife."

I answered, "Yes, Sir" as I waited for him to continue.

"Reverend Cole, I saw the look on you and your wife's faces as you left the Custer Colt in my hands. I felt that you were both giving up a dear old friend and it has bothered me a great deal since, so I contacted Colt Manufacturing and they have created an exact firing replica of the old revolver. The new piece is bright, shiny, and made of the finest firearm material available today. You could use this one in combat and not have to worry about the metal exploding if it were loaded with the wrong ammunition. The only difference from the original is the serial number. The numerals 130175 are the same; however, a zero has been placed before the first numeral because it is a special, one-of-a-kind reproduction, and the manufacture date on the barrel is the current date. The holster, belt, and cartridge case has been exactly copied also. I realize a

111

copy of the old Colt will never replace the original in your hearts and minds, but perhaps it will be a reminder of the weapon that played such a role in your family's history."

He said a few more things, but my mind had wandered into thoughts of things the colonel would never know, and my heart felt full.

As I said thank you, my thoughts continued. *The gift is great, but the general and his friendship can never be replaced.*

After a few more courtesies in both directions, the call came to an end.

The colonel had also said the package would be delivered by special courier in a couple of days. Two days later a military sedan pulled up in front of the parsonage and a top kick sergeant came to the door carrying a fine leather case and an oblong cardboard box.

After an exchange of salutes, with me not in uniform, just in my rough old work clothes, the sergeant presented me with the leather case and cardboard box.

As he returned to the car, I carried the two packages into my small office, sat down at my desk, and slowly opened the leather case. As tears flooded my eyes, I saw the new general in all his glory before me. It was in every respect a perfect copy of the old Colt exactly as it looked all the time before we took it to the Point. As my hand touched the wooden grips, a small sound of surprise escaped my lips. I felt warmth, and the weapon leaped into my hand. Then I saw it. In the same black ink script on the satin liner of the handmade leather case were the words, "Brothers in arms for life." And then the script continued, "As long as you live, I will stand shoulder to shoulder with you in combat. G. A. C. " As I read the script a second time it slowly faded until it disappeared.

Suddenly a feeling of joy swept over me, but at the same time there was a much deeper feeling of, "What's happening?" We took Custer's spirit to West Point and suddenly it had returned to Ellie and me. All I could suppose was that Custer's spirit knew something we did not know.

Continuing to wonder, I placed the reproduction back into the case and closed the lid. After a while I opened the cardboard box and found an exact copy of the original holster, belt, and cartridge case.

Another question, how do I explain this to Ellie?

Ellie was fascinated by the new revelation, but the same as I, she said, "What does it mean? We returned the general to the Point as he requested, but he's still with us."

I answered, "We'll just have to wait and see. I'm sure an answer will come when the time is right."

Chapter 31

Behind the church along Rumble Creek was a patch of uninhabited timber, so I decided to take the new Colt reproduction out for a little test firing. I had not fired a handgun since my departure from the service. Custer's spirit had fired the old Colt once defending the church, but my finger had not pulled a trigger in some years.

I found a large pine with a clear view toward it from about seventy good long strides away. I tacked a paper target on the old pine about five feet up from the ground. Then I loaded six fresh cartridges into the cylinder. I positioned myself facing slightly left with the target off my right shoulder. I raised the new Colt with the muzzle slightly above the target and started to settle into a relaxed firing pose. Suddenly the muzzle dropped to the center of the target and all six rounds exploded from the barrel in about two or three seconds. Then I felt or heard a soft belly laugh as the new reproduction dangled from my hand, muzzle pointed toward the ground. The paper target hanging from the bark of the old pine appeared to be torn into shreds.

Then I also heard a soft tinkling sound almost like a small silver bell, a young women's giggle. When I caught my breath, I strolled down to look closer at the target. The target had six neatly spaced holes in it forming a number seven. Then I realized what the laughter meant. Custer had fired the new Colt, but what was the giggling sound?

115

And then I knew. Custer and his lady love had both come to visit.

I couldn't help myself. I cried. But at the same time, I thanked God for his infinite grace.

I was both thrilled and experiencing a feeling of pain for my old friend. I took him home to the Point, but was he still forced to be attached to me? Would he and Libby ever be free from the curse of the old Colt? Then at the base of the big pine I saw the beautiful bloom of a white rose. It wasn't growing, just a large blossom lying there. All I could do was wonder why.

I tacked up a second target, reloaded the new general, and fired six shots of my own. All six were in the target, but I knew I could never match the prowess of the boy general.

I gathered the rose and my things, then walked back to the parsonage to show Ellie and discuss with her the latest happenings.

Chapter 32

As I opened my eyes I felt rested and relaxed. It was early in the morning, and I was looking forward to making great progress in many of the tasks I planned to face during the day. I rolled over and discovered that Ellie was not next to me in bed. Knowing it was about her delivery time, I quickly arose and went into the bathroom to see if she was there. Not finding her in the bath I headed for the kitchen, where I found her talking on the phone to Effie and heard her tell her grandmother she thought it was time but wasn't sure.

I broke into their conversation and asked what was wrong. Ellie said, "Pains are coming about fifteen minutes apart."

I asked, "Don't you think it's time to call Doctor Backster?"

"I don't know. I've never done this before."

Then I heard Effie speaking loud enough for me to hear her voice from the phone. "Get her to the clinic. Now!" I took the receiver from Ellie's hand and answered, "I agree. We'll call you as soon as we see the doctor and know something."

"No you won't. I'll be meeting you there." Then Effie hung up.

I helped Ellie get dressed in some loose sweats and we were out the door. When we arrived at the clinic, attendants were waiting in the parking lot with a wheelchair. Doctor

117

Backster was also waiting. Effie had called him the moment she hung up and he had arrived just a few seconds later.

In less than forty-five minutes George Samuel Cole was born at 6:55 in the morning, January 17, 1990. The general's first prophesy had come to reality.

The doctor announced that both mother and child were healthy and well. The only exception was the baby had a small medical instrument mark in the shape of a small number seven on his left hip, but he felt it would fade from view in a couple of days. I was fairly positive it would also, perhaps even a lot quicker. Later when I opened the leather pistol case to clean and fondle the reproduction Colt, I found an eagle feather with red velvet wrapping around its lower tip, a young brave's first headdress feather. I felt deep pride, but at the same time I hoped my son would never have to become a warrior. I hoped three generations of Coles serving in the armed services of the United States for one hundred years was enough.

After the appropriate time Ellie and George were released from the clinic and the Cole household was finally a complete family, mother, father, and child. Though Ellie and I were first-time parents at an older-than-usual age, we believed we could be good parents with God's help and direction, so with that belief and faith we continued to trundle on.

Chapter 33

Baby George had barely been weaned and cut a few teeth when Ellie and I got a second family surprise. During one of their checkups Dr. Backster informed Ellie she was expecting again. Ellie may not have been the happiest woman on receiving that news, but for me it was another grand bit of God's grace I was to be given. I loved Ellie and dearly loved this latest gift we had created, and I was fairly certain it would be another male child, a second little brave, so to speak.

David Armstrong Cole arrived at his appointed time, May 5, 1991, and a second eagle feather appeared in the pistol case, this one with blue velvet wrapping. No other evidence of our resident spirit made itself known during the period of the two births, but I was sure a proud uncle and perhaps aunt were in attendance, as the general and Libby never had children of their own.

David's first name was given in honor of Ellie's father, David Wadsworth Stokes, and the second name was given to once more honor the general.

George's and David's births coming so close together quickly gave rise to a very serious problem—room! Where could we put David to sleep? The parsonage was so small that George had been sleeping in our bedroom in a very small crib, but there was not enough room for a second crib, so David had to sleep in a car carrier. Ellie and I immediately began the search for a larger house, one we could afford. We decided we would try to purchase, not rent.

One evening, as we were fighting that storm, Effie invited us for an evening meal and to discuss our home-buying efforts. That little pause in our hectic routine was greatly appreciated. The meal was southern cuisine at its finest—fried chicken, green beans and almonds with bacon seasoning, grilled potatoes, garden green salad, honey-dipped cornbread, iced tea, and hot coffee. Oh yes, and deep-dish apple pie with homemade ice cream.

After the fine meal Ellie and Effie cleared the table and washed dishes. Then for a few minutes they fed the little guys and prepared them for bed. After they were down, the three of us settled down for a nice conversation while the two little ones slept in their car seats. The subject of discussion was how the Coles could find a new home.

Effie broke out in a huge smile as she made the opening statement, "Ellie, Jim, I just may have located a house in your price range and close to the church." With puzzlement in my voice and frustration in my being, I queried, "Where and who? We've looked everywhere around close, and there's nothing available."

After a slight pause to build up suspense and anticipation, she announced, "Right here!"

Ellie questioned, "What do you mean, right here?"

This time Effie grinned as she said, "My house. I'm old, and sometime in the near future I will need nursing care, or I will be gone. Ellie, you already know that when I'm gone you will inherit this house and everything else I own. So why not inherit the house now when you need it?" Before Ellie or I could say anything, she continued. "Ellie, remember the servants' quarters behind this place? You surely remember when I had them renovated with the intent to rent them, but then I never did. They're ultramodern now, really nicer than this house. This monster, with six rooms down and five up would be more than enough for the four of you and enough more in case more little ones come along.

I had heard around town the stories of the Broyles-Stokes mansion and other holdings but had never given any of it much thought. I assumed there were many heirs to Effie's estate, so I spoke up.

"Effie, what about other heirs? What you are proposing would not be fair to the others."

Effie gave forth with a small giggle. "Jim, Ellie, you, and your children are all the heirs there are. I was an only child, and only had one child, Ellie's deceased father, and Ellie is an only child, so she gets it all. Ellie and I have kept her birthright a secret to ward off gold-digging men. Her first husband found out somehow that in the future she would inherit a little wealth and began to pressure her to demand it immediately. That's why she divorced him before you came along. But we both discovered that the Reverend Cole was just who he said he was and has proven it over the past years. And now there is a whole Cole family to enjoy that inheritance. So I want you and Ellie to take the house, live in it, and have the good life. Now if you will both look closely, you'll see that I've already moved my personal effects into the servants' quarters, so as soon as tomorrow the four of you can start moving in."

I had cried when my men were killed because of grief. At that moment I cried because of gratitude.

Moving into the Stokes mansion was no small task, but with the assistance of many church members the work was accomplished in a few days. However, it was determined that the parsonage house would remain, at least for a time, as only a larger office space for church business. I would not have to handle church affairs from my home because the total church office would be right next door to the church. Ellie and I could check in on Effie daily and assure she was happy, content, and safe in the smaller quarters more appropriate for her age, and George and David would enjoy the roomier area for play.

As the weeks, months, and years passed by, the Cole family became more and more content being residents of the small confines of Rumble Creek.

Occasionally I would take the new general out for a firing exercise, and the spirit always made our visits complete by demonstrating his pistol-firing abilities as I had to bear the embarrassing female giggles for being the lesser shot.

Sometimes I wondered about the third coin and if it was a prophecy of a Cole daughter? I finally decided if that was not what the coin meant and there was no daughter, life was already more than very special with two beautiful sons.

Chapter 34

With a house, family, and plenty of room to grow, life was extremely pleasurable, and I was happy with my daily routine.

One morning as I was leisurely involved in some rough-and-tumble play with George and David, the phone rang and Ellie was not close enough to answer it, so I extracted myself from the grip of my two sons and attended to the detail. As I heard the person on the other end of the line say hello, I believed the voice to be vaguely familiar but could not place the person who was speaking.

"Hello, Captain Cole. Sorry, Reverend Cole, Colonel Murry here."

My mind quickly engaged and I replied, "Good morning, Colonel. Great to hear your voice. What can I do for you this morning?"

"No, it's what I can do for you. A few years back while you were visiting us, before you left the Point you made a request that if more information came to light about Custer or the weapon to let you know. There's no new information, but something odd has happened here that I thought you might find amusing. Because of all the new interest in Custer and his wife caused by the display of the old Colt, our groundskeeper decided to dress up his and Libby's graves. He planted a red rosebush on George's grave and a white rosebush on Libby's to represent love and purity between the two. Immediately the bushes began to grow toward each other and became entwined.

No matter how hard the gardener works the bushes cannot be kept apart."

As he chuckled, the colonel continued. "Sounds like some kind of wild love story, and it's a cute tale, don't you think?"

I answered the colonel as honestly as I could, remembering the general's request to be taken to the Point to be with Libby. Then I knew.

"Colonel, everything I have ever read about General Custer stated that he dearly loved Libby, and she loved him just as dearly. Perhaps their spirits are so happy to be together after her death that they will never ever be kept apart."

I thanked the colonel for the message, and we continued to talk awhile longer about the great new interest in Custer, evidently brought on by the new display of the Long Colt.

As I hung up the phone and returned to David and George, my heart was filled with love for the general and his lady. Then I knew what the white rose bloom I found at the foot of the old pine represented—the boy general and Libby together forever, doing all the things a loving couple desire to do. Ellie's and my question was completely answered. The general was finally and completely free, and the old Colt had returned to being nothing more than an oddity of history and an instrument of battle. I had to believe him staying near was a sign of his promised friendship for eternity.

Chapter 35

After we moved into our new house, our lives were idyllic for a few quiet years. The Cole family members were all happy, healthy, and growing in age and God's will. My pastorate almost ceased to seem laborious. I believed that God had singled me out to live in His grace for the rest of my life, but I was soon to have my faith tested once again.

Midway through the second week of a beautiful month of early fall, I awoke to a mild morning with the promise of a warm to hot afternoon. I had just begun putting the finishing touches on my sermon for the following Sunday but stopped and sat down to enjoy a second cup of coffee. Picking up my steaming cup, I decided to move out onto the front porch to enjoy a few tranquil moments.

Mrs. Forbish, who lived next door, suddenly burst out of her front door wringing her hands and screaming, "They've blown up the towers! God help us, they've blown up the towers!"

I knew something dreadful had happened, but I couldn't imagine what Mrs. Forbish was screaming about. I quickly jumped up from my chair and ran next door to see if I could help. As I reached her front steps, the poor woman noticed my arrival and ran to me, continuing to scream. "Brother Jeremiah, please pray for the souls of all those poor people who have been killed in New York City."

I asked, "Sister, what people who have been killed, and how?"

125

"Brother Jeremiah, someone has flown two big passenger planes into the twin skyscrapers in New York City, and hundreds, maybe thousands, of people have been killed." I immediately dropped my head, and with Mrs. Forbish and I holding hands, prayed to God for mercy and guidance. By the time I said amen the street was full of people discussing what disaster had just befallen our country.

Later, as the radio and TV told the story in a more complete fashion, I realized that type of activity would probably lead to more war, perhaps even World War III. As I watched the TV, I began to pray for all the young men and women in our armed forces and at the same time began to worry about my two sons becoming of military age before a Third World War would even end.

Chapter 36

In a few days we learned it was a terrorist attack by a foreign power, but not a foreign country. A force of radical Islamic Muslims financed by a wealthy Saudi family member planned and executed an attack, taking down the twin commercial towers in New York City using two large loaded passenger planes as bombs. And within a short time, a third plane crashed into the Pentagon and another was forced to crash in an open field in Pennsylvania, when the passengers overpowered the muslim attackers. The loss of innocent lives from the four horrors numbered in the thousands.

Needless to say, my military training and background caused my mind to snap to attention and I became madder than hell! Then all I could do was pray for God to understand. *Please God, forgive my words and thoughts, but I cannot forgive such actions.*

Because the attack happened on Tuesday, I had almost a full week to establish another sermon condemning such godless action. I was so enraged that God's holy words could not cool my desire for revenge. On Sunday morning my sermon was a hot-blooded condemnation of all things muslim. I knew the words I was preaching were not God's words, but unchecked hatred leaking from the very depth of my soul. I felt I would never be forgiven, but I could not help myself.

Sadly, being in a southern state deep in the Bible belt, my ranting was readily received, so for several Sundays I continued to center my attacks on those responsible for the 9-11 attack.

Evidently my conviction was so strong that some news organizations across the nation picked up on what I was preaching and I gained national attention. Being a disabled veteran turned pulpit preacher caught the spirit of the country and I became a backwash celebrity. But in some parts of the country and by certain elements of society I was condemned for what I was preaching. I ignored that segment of our population and continued on with my sermons of total displeasure and hate.

While I was so heavily distracted by what I thought and how I was reacting, Ellie became ill. Then fear struck me like a lightning bolt. Had I challenged God to such an extent that I was now in line for his punishment? The real hurt was that he would lay the pain on Ellie for my transgressions. I was scared beyond any fear I had ever known. Ellie and the boys were my whole life and now I had awakened God's wrath. All I could do was beg for God's forgiveness or punishment for me, not Ellie. For several days I hid myself from the world and prayed for God to release Ellie from my sins. Her health was all I could think about.

Thankfully it was finally determined she was once more pregnant. I immediately fell down and thanked God for his forgiveness, but at the same time I was still terribly concerned about the direction the United States was being driven and how it would affect my children.

Chapter 37

Sometime later as I was opening the afternoon mail I came upon a strange envelope. It had been mailed from a small town in the state of California. The address was very strange and caused me to be a little concerned. The address was as follows:

From:
>A very concerned Believer
>Cable, California 95401

To:
>A Warrior of the State turned Preacher
>Baptist Church of Rumble Creek
>1000 Rumble Creek
>Rumble River, AL 35543

The message:

>Dear Infidel Preacher,
>
>As a follower of the true God of Earth, Allah, I pray you and your congregation a swift and timely demise. You and yours have been chosen by the True Believers to be used as an example to demonstrate to all who question the true power of Allah.

Your head will be harvested and displayed as a trophy in Allah's name. Your congregation will be wiped from the face of the earth and your church will be burned out of existence. You and yours have only one recourse. You must convert or be eliminated.

A True Believer

It was only after I had read the letter that I happened to think there might have been poison on the paper. I guessed I would find out soon enough. The passage of time proved there was not.

When I first received the letter, I simply filed it away and decided it was a crank letter, but as time went on, we began to hear of actual attacks on people here at home by radical believers.

Then the church or I received a simple postcard that had just a few words on it. "Your time is growing short."

It was mailed from upstate New York. After that little wakeup call, I quickly became concerned for my family and my parishioners. I called a meeting of the deacons and elders to explain the threats and my concerns. A few of the church members said, "A crank, just ignore it." Some others said, "Maybe we had better close the church and hold no services for a while and maybe it will cool down." However, the majority of deacons, elders, and members asked, "Is there any way to defend ourselves if an attack is made?"

Being a past US Army officer and a veteran combat commander, I knew any attempt at self-defense would be extremely dangerous and perhaps very foolhardy, but the majority of the church members continued to challenge me to prepare a defense for the old church and the congregation.

I decided no matter what might come I was determined to be a little prepared immediately. My first order of defense was the Long Colt in the floor safe. I decided to have it on my person as much as I could in case a lone attacker made an attempt on me, my family, or any of the church members.

As I removed the leather case from the small safe, a strange feeling came over me. A sense of strength and resolve caused me to believe that responsible people could overcome almost any challenge, and I resolved to face the problem head-on. When I opened the case, I discovered a piece of what appeared to be the remains of an antique military unit banner fairly covered with dried blood. Through the brown stains I could make out a numeral 7. As I looked closer at a spot that was free of stain I saw a familiar black script that said, "I would gladly die a second time to help defend you, your family, and the rights of your people." As soon as I read the script and understood what it said, the cloth burst into flames and burned to ashes. However, nothing else around the small fire was even slightly scorched.

At once I knew the general would be at my side throughout any terrorist activities.

I took the Colt out of the case, loaded five of the cylinder's chambers, lowered the hammer on the empty chamber, and slipped the weapon into my waistband. I immediately felt prepared to stand for my church.

Chapter 38

Over the next few days I prayed and planned. Then I revised my plans and continued to pray. As I was deep in trying to imagine various attack scenarios, I was interrupted by a visit from Effie.

"Jim, is it possible for a bunch of old fools to stand against an attack by an organized band of religious radicals?"

I thought for a moment before I attempted to answer her question, but suddenly I felt something causing me to ask her a question before I answered hers.

"Effie, why are you asking such a question?"

"Many of your church members are talking about arming themselves and attempting to ambush anyone or any group that tries to make a move on our church or congregation. I thought you might have some idea if their idea is just plain crazy."

"Effie, it might be possible if some things are done beforehand to prepare for an attack and if everyone understands the extreme danger involved."

"If we decided to do what was necessary, would you lead and direct us?"

"I would be a proud and willing commander of such an army of the Lord."

"Then get to commanding because more than seventy-five percent of the parish members are willing to fight and die, if necessary, to defend our church and pastor."

Hearing that from Effie caused me to believe our congregation was determined to stand up for their faith and convictions. If that were the case, I knew I had to protect them in every way I could. As I continued to consider the situation, securing the buildings and grounds was the most prudent place to start. After a meeting of the possible combatants, the decision was made to continue with a planned defense. Immediately all windows at ground level were treated to make them bulletproof. The outside doors, including the small basement's furnace room and coal-bin doors, were reinforced with steel. The old coal chute had been closed and sealed years before so it was not an issue. The old coal bin was now used for church equipment storage. Last on the security list was a closed-circuit TV network. The cameras covered all of the rooms outside the main hall and the entire perimeter of the building, concentrating on the parking lot and any blind spots. The multi-screen monitor for the closed-circuit system was built into the base of my pulpit podium, with a second cable hookup to the computer in the office.

While security was being updated, I took all the members who wanted to be involved out back into the pines, and I taught and they practiced weapon handling. Being old country boys and girls, many of them were already fairly accurate shots with long weapons, rifles, and shotguns, but I felt handguns would be better suited for action inside a building. My plans were to force attackers to enter the church where it would be easier to spring an ambush, so we also began to assemble a selection of pistols of different sizes for both men and women. In a couple of weeks most of the members felt they could handle a pistol, and most could hit a man-size target at about thirty to fifty feet. The women had small-caliber weapons and the men larger, more potent calibers.

Next, I laid out a seating placement in the church sanctuary forming a cross-fire pattern, placing the better shots in the most strategic places. Those locations became their assigned positions during every church service.

We then worked up a set of signals I could direct from the pulpit that would alert all the members in attendance that an attack was imminent. When a certain signal was given the members would simply sink to the floor between the pews, allowing the shooters open lanes of fire in all directions. Like any good training, practice sessions were held. I gave the signal and the shooters assumed their firing positions while the rest of the members disappeared to the floor. I even pulled some unannounced practice during regular services and the moves were made flawlessly.

I continued to pray that we would never need to use the scheme, but I believed if we needed to, we were ready.

Chapter 39

Near the first week in May, 2003, things were hectic. Ellie's third pregnancy was pure pain and anguish. She and I realized we were both reaching the extreme end of our childbearing years, but a baby girl had become our fondest dream. And when the general made his apparent prophesy, we hoped that was what he meant, and we hoped and prayed it would happen.

And yes, this time we knew for sure she was carrying a female child. The ultrasound test had already revealed the truth, so Ellie was willing to bear the discomfort for the birth to happen. With her delivery date being very close, it was horrible.

At the same time, there were some mysterious happenings that I could not explain. Some of the security equipment began to do things on its own. Once during a service all the video cameras came on at one time and the monitors displayed old western movies of cowboys and Indians, but the professional technicians could find nothing wrong in the system.

With all the pressure, I decided to take the Colt out behind the church for a little recreational shooting. I guess the general decided to play some jokes because every shot I fired hit the pine tree and fell to the ground. However, it was odd I never heard or sensed his laughter. He never indicated he was even around. When I returned the pistol to the leather case, the cavity for the Colt was full of dead

137

leaves. I was a little fearful and didn't feel that trick was funny. Then I wondered if it was some kind of warning.

It had been about eight or so months since I received the letter and postcard, so by 2003 I had decided it was a crank. But was it? To be on the safe side I held a couple more practice sessions for defense of the church. Quickly the congregation returned to the level of preparedness they had demonstrated months before, so I was confident the church was well protected.

As we counted down the hours to Ellie's due date, I asked Effie to stay with us day and night in the big house in case of emergencies. The boys also needed some support. George was the old man of the house at the age of thirteen and David was his main aid at almost twelve. With their able assistance I was permitted to carry out my preaching duties quite well.

Saturday night of May 3, 2003, Ellie was very uncomfortable. She was sure that baby Libby would arrive within maybe a couple of hours.

The whole family decided she would honor her great-grandmother's name and also the Custer family's female name as Effinetta Elizabeth "Libby" Cole. The boys knew the basis of their names, favoring the old Colt's history in our family, as did Effie, but Ellie was the only one other than I who knew the whole story of the spirit.

Saturday night I told the boys if the baby did not arrive by church time the next morning, I wanted them to stay home with their mom and grandma to be of help, if needed, and I would go on to church and hold service. I also called Dr. Backster and told him what was happening. He said he would stay prepared until the baby was delivered.

About ten o'clock that night we all went to bed in hopes Ellie could settle down a little bit and sleep. For whatever reason, she had a peaceful night, but strangely I caught the scent of burning sage and felt a cool breeze carrying the smell of mountain pine through our bedroom all night.

Because Ellie was resting, I arose early, showered, got dressed, and walked the block or so to the church. I checked out security, turned on the TV system, and retrieved the new general from the safe in the old parsonage. I placed the Colt under the towel on the lectern and looked at the displays on the monitors. Everything was working perfectly.

I gathered my sermon material from my briefcase and stood at the lectern as I once more scanned my notes. My sermon was also in perfect order. I was ready to preach.

Then for some reason I checked the new general once more. *The grips were not warm, they were hot! The general was there in full readiness.* I was fearful and surprised at the same time. What did it mean? And then it dawned on me. Libby was going to be born today and he was there for the event. I relaxed as I realized he was telling me he was my number-one support. I touched the piece once more and thanked him for his friendship. Then I continued on with the service preparation.

Chapter 40

I wandered around through the church as I waited for service time to arrive. I had heard nothing from home, so I assumed that Ellie and the baby were okay and Effie, George, and David had everything under control.

Finally, the service hour arrived and with it the congregation, in ones, twos, threes, and groups. I noticed everyone moved to their assigned security positions and visually checked their assigned firing areas. I was very pleased.

I moved to the pulpit and assumed my position behind the lectern.

The service began with a short prayer and then one of the old hymns, "The Old Rugged Cross."

For some reason I couldn't explain, I looked down at the toe of my shoe and saw on one of the monitor screens movement in the parking lot. As I concentrated on the screen, I saw four large sedans in a line down the middle of the lot. Then a back door of one opened and a figure all in black stepped out onto the gravel. In his hand I saw a short automatic weapon. By that time four men had exited each of the four vehicles and started walking toward the front door. Then I observed one man of the group was dressed in a white robe and wearing a colored head covering. The rest had their faces hidden by tightly knitted coverings with only holes for their eyes. The man in white headed for the back of the church. I knew both back and front doors were unlocked, so all I could do was give the

141

signal for an imminent attack. As if by magic most of the members disappeared from sight and the rest produced their weapons and assumed their firing positions.

The first intruder into the sanctuary pointed his weapon at the ceiling and fired several rounds, while reciting some muslim chant. I supposed his action was to scare and intimidate the parishioners. The other fourteen fanned out around the back of the hall, but instead of fear gripping the crowd, a wall of fire erupted from around the room and most of the gunmen went down.

The one who had fired the first shots into the ceiling dropped to his knees behind the back pew, leaned forward over the pew, and aimed his weapon at me as I stood at the podium. Below his chin I saw a gnarled old hand rise up and place the business end of a small silver-colored revolver under his chin and I heard the pop of a small-caliber round being discharged. The attacker stood straight up and collapsed to the floor behind the pew. I knew that was Mr. Foster's regular seat. He was one of the oldest members and a local hero of service in the Second World War. He had several medals to verify his status.

As I continued to watch, I saw that only about two or three of the attackers were still standing after the initial volley, but they suddenly threw down their firearms and ran back out the front door of the church. Almost immediately I heard the sound of an auto engine being heavily gunned and the sound of gravel being violently disturbed.

But then my memory snapped, and I remembered the man in the white robe and the colored headdress. I grabbed the new general from under the towel and spun around to face the back hall. Before I could focus on the back entry, my eyes registered the icon of Christ on the cross hanging on the wall behind the podium. I remembered my military oath to defend my country and its constitution even unto death. Could I profess to be a defender of God and His teachings and not be willing to die in His service? I steeled myself to whatever was to come. As my eyes caught movement, I realized my turn to the rear entry was too late! The man in white had his automatic weapon trained on the upper portion of my body. Then I saw the muzzle flash of his rifle being fired.

"Allahu Akbar!" I heard him scream in a short burst of breath, as I felt the shock of several bullets hitting me in the chest and stomach. But I was surprised that I felt no pain. Then I saw a look of utter terror in the attacker's eyes as he dropped his weapon, threw up his hands, and commenced clawing the empty air above his head. He violently struggled for a minute or two and crumpled to the floor.

Then I looked down at my chest and ran my left hand over my chest and stomach. I was covered in blood, but I still felt no pain. I also saw I was still holding the new general in my right hand, but I couldn't recall firing a single round.

As I stood there, I also couldn't understand how I could be so badly wounded and still standing. Then I thought, Am I a ghost? Am I dead and don't know it?

I looked down once more at my body wounds and saw that I was dressed in a fringed deerskin jacket.

Below the waist I saw blue woolen trousers with a gold stripe down the leg, and I was wearing cavalry boots.

Suddenly, I knew what had happened. Custer's spirit had surrounded me, and he truly was killed a second time defending me and my church.

But what happened to the attacker in white? I couldn't believe I had shot him. Maybe one of the other members shot him.

I looked down at my lower body one more time, and there was no blood. I was dressed once more in my own clothing.

I quickly turned back toward the pews and loudly asked, "Was anyone hurt or killed in the attack?" After a long moment I learned no one suffered even a scratch.

Then I turned and walked over to the man in white. I was fairly certain he was dead, but I saw no blood nor any wounds. I thought he must have died of a heart attack because no bullet ever touched him. Then I felt the new general warm in my hand, and as I looked down toward the .45 I saw the monitors at my feet. On one of the screens was a recording from some old movie of Custer strangling an Indian warrior who was covered in white war paint and wearing a colored headdress. I only saw the tape for a moment before the screen faded. Then I knew what had happened.

I dropped my head and said a silent prayer, giving thanks for such a friend. As I raised my head, I became aware that there were state police all around me and throughout the church.

I learned very quickly the man in white was a foreign radical whom the US government had been looking for after he entered the country illegally. The rest of the band was made up of homegrown radicals. One of the men shot in the initial volley was still alive, and the commander of the state police felt he would tell the entire story.

We of the church did not have to tell our story as the state law enforcement was aware of all I had been involved in while in the military and as a civilian. So I asked if I could put the general away. As the Colt had not been fired and I had the necessary paperwork to prove ownership, my request was honored. I excused myself and walked next door to the old parsonage and opened the leather case to put the big pistol away. There in the cavity was a single, tiny, handmade gold-star necklace charm strung on a yellow silk ribbon, and on the lining of the case in black script were the words, "Congratulations, Reverend, on the birth of your daughter!" Once again, as soon as I read the words, they faded.

Chapter 41

I realized that Libby must have already been delivered, so I rushed to put the Colt away and then ran out the door to head for the hospital. But as I exited the door Effie and the boys were there to greet me. George grabbed my hand and began to shake it like a grown man as we greeted each other. Then he said, "Daddy we have a new girl in the family and she is David's and my sister. And Mom let David and me tell the doctor what her name would be and why."

I may have embarrassed them both, but I kissed my boys on the head and silently thanked God one more time for giving them to Ellie and me.

In a short time the four of us had walked to the hospital. First, I rushed into Ellie's room to see her and tell her that everything and everyone was okay, in case she had heard about the attack. And I thanked her for giving me a little princess. Later I would tell her about the spirit and his part in overcoming the attack.

Ellie was still groggy so I didn't stay long. After a kiss and a pat on the hand, I moved on to see our new daughter.

I felt Libby Cole would live up to her namesake as she cried louder than all the other babies in the nursery, but she quieted down when the nurse let me touch her for the first time. As I held her, I became aware of a couple somewhere close by, laughing and giggling, though I saw no one.

Then I realized who! The spirits of the adopted aunt and uncle had come all the way from West Point to see their new niece.

After I finished my visit I asked Effie to see the boys home as I needed to walk, think, and clear my head of all that had happened this fourth day of May, 2003. She understood and said she would see that they arrived at the house safely.

As I started placing one foot in front of the other moving along the street, I allowed my mind to rethink all the previous hours.

Did Custer's spirit use some old Indian remedy to allow Ellie to rest all night? I believed I smelled the scent of the Bighorn Mountains in our bedroom. I also believed he wrapped me in his spirit as the attack was taking place and took the bullets that were meant for me and killed the foreign radical. Either the general strangled the man to death or he allowed his apparition, the one Ellie saw, to appear and his scalped countenance to be seen, scaring the radical leader to death.

I was almost positive the odd happenings earlier that week were meant as a warning of the upcoming attack.

I completely understood the birth gifts for the two boys. Both would become warriors of some type in their own rights. And I believed I understood Libby's birth gift, or most of it. The gold star was a general's star, perhaps one of his own. But I wasn't absolutely sure of the yellow ribbon. Then, just like a whistling breeze in the distance, I once again heard the strains of "Garry Owen," and I hummed along to the old 7th Cavalry's marching tune. Then suddenly the band broke into a livelier beat and I recognized the refrain of "She Wore a Yellow Ribbon," another old cavalry marching song, and I knew what the yellow ribbon meant. My princess would always be protected by the spirit of the historic commander of the 7th Cavalry regiment of the US Army.

I said a prayer asking God's blessing for the general and our friendship, then turned, brought my body to full attention, and snapped my most formal salute in the direction of the sounds as they wafted away on the cool spring breeze.

Once more I bowed my head and gave thanks to God for his eternal grace and my salvation, for my family and church. Then I also prayed peace would prevail, that mankind would cease having deadly hatred for different skin colors, different faiths, and different national origins.

As I raised my head toward the heavens, I observed an apparition of a lone cavalry trooper on horseback fading into the distant clouds. He had flowing yellow hair and was wearing a fringed buckskin jacket.

Though I never knew him in life, just knowing him in spirit made me feel so happy and fulfilled.

As I continued on toward home, I once more whispered another quiet prayer. "God, allow the boy general and his bride to rest in peace from this day forward for all eternity."

Genealogical Chronology of James Riley Cole

Samuel Doyle Cole 1849-1923

Born in the spring of 1849 near Boonville, Missouri
Joined the US Army in 1866
Assigned to Custer's Army circa 1873
Missed massacre in 1876
Acquired Long Colt after Custer's death, in 1876
    (27 years old)
Married Maggie Jane Riley 1898
Male child born in 1900 (51 years old)
Died in 1923 (74 years old)

James Riley Cole 1900-1980

Born 1900 near Boonville, Missouri
Joined the US Army (18 years old)
In France until end of First World War
    (Carried the old Colt)
Married Wendy Wiley Wells in 1946
Male child, son, born in 1947 (47 years old)
Died in 1980 (80 years old)

Genealogical Chronology of James Riley Cole
(Continued)

James Riley Cole Jr. 1947-?

Captain in the US Army in 1973 in Vietnam
(26 years old) (carried old Colt)
Injured in combat 1974 (27 years old)
Lost in life for about four years (31 years old)
Started preaching about 1979 (32 years old)
Black problems started in mid 1960s and carried on
for some years.
Racial problem hit his church in early 1980s
(Almost 36 years old)
Met Ellie Mae Stokes Duren in 1981
(She was 26 years old, he was 34 years old)
Finally married Ellie in 1985
(He was 38 years old, she was 30)
Fear of more racial problems in 1986
Birth of George Samuel Cole, January 17, 1990
(James age 43, and Ellie age 35)
Birth of David Armstrong Cole, May 5, 1991
(James age 44, and Ellie age 36)
9-11 happens in 2001
(James is 54 years old, and Ellie age 46 years old)
Attack on church May 4, 2003
(James age 56 years old, and Ellie age 48 years old)
Birth of Effinetta Elizabeth "Libby" Cole, May 4, 2003
(George Samuel age 13, and David age almost 12;
Effinetta Ann Broyles Stokes [Effie] age 85)

About the Author

Roger Baker retired from teaching school after twenty-nine years of service.

During his career in education. he used storytelling as a means to enrich his classroom presentations and capture the attention of his students.

He has been spending leisure hours of his retirement with storytelling, now with his pen.

He and his wife reside in central Missouri. He has one previously published book, *Two for the Price*.